FREERUNNER

A YOUNG ADULT NOVEL

KATHY CASSEL

[HPP]

Haven Point Publishing, Lynn Haven, FL
Freerunner
Copyright © 2022 by Kathy Cassel

Cover and Interior Design: Diana L. Sharples
PUBLISHED BY: Haven Point Publishing, Lynn Haven, FL

Paperback ISBN: 979-8-9859043-2-1
Ebook ISBN: 979-8-9859043-1-4

Summary: Set against the backdrop of the sport of freerunning, Kiana Scott must decide whether she will continue running or face her past abuser in order to save a child from the things she endured.

Coming of age fiction, child molestation fiction, family relationships fiction, freerunning fiction, track and field fiction, friendship fiction.

Endorsements for Freerunner

A Selah Award finalist

Kathy Cassel weaves a fast-paced, insightful, coming of age narrative that is not only engaging, tragic and full of emotional turmoil but also explores second chances and renewed faith.

Jeanne DeAngulo
veteran middle school/high school teacher

From the first paragraph, I was hooked by Cassel's true-to-life story of teen "misfits" who find escape through freerunning. This action-packed tale of friendship and hope will capture even the most reluctant reader.

Lori Ewart
Veteran high school/junior high English teacher
and young people's librarian

Kathy Cassel has long had a sincere heart for teens. Her writing proves it.

In Freerunner, a teen girl is mixed up in more than one way and goes through several phases of difficult emotions. Young adult readers will enjoy entering Kiana (Kia, "like the car") Scott's mind as she deals with some pretty tough issues.

It's a great read filled with life lessons that will remain with the reader for a very long time. I highly recommend Freerunner.

Katara Washington Patton
Author of *Inspiration for Christian Teen Girls*

The first chapter swept me into the storyline, soon revealing the main character's pain, and her reason for freerunning.

Joan C. Benson
Author of *His Gift*

Freerunner is written in a realistic way that offers hope and healing for the children impacted. I highly endorse this book.

Felicia Melville
Therapeutic foster parent

This story tackles tough issues with fast-paced action and suspense. The characters quickly come alive and you feel like you know them. Woven into the plot are unexpected twists and turns that make this story a great read. This is one of those books that's hard to put down because you can't wait to see what will happen next. Great for teens, but adults as well.

Crystal Bowman
best selling, award-winning author
of more than 100 books.

There are those rare, magic moments when you pick up a book, read the first few lines and immediately know you've found a gem. Freerunner is one of those stories.

T.E. Bradford
Author of the Divide Series
and Six World Saga books.

A strong plot, unique characters, and deft airing of an oft-hidden issue, childhood sexual abuse, make this a young-adult book you'll devour in one sitting.

Phyllis Wheeler
Author of The Long Shadow.

Dedication:

Kia's story is dedicated to all who are still running from the things that haunt them. It is my prayer that this book will help you run into the future and all you are meant to be.

Acknowledgments

A special thank you to Jeanette Windle who believed in this book and guided me in bringing Kia to life.

Also a special thanks to my husband, Rick, and our children who believed in this book and encouraged me in the writing of it.

And to Diana Sharples for her cover design

Chapter One

Night is my favorite time of day. Night's when I can be anonymous, swallowed by darkness, when I run to outdistance the voices in my head and the images that are never far away.

As I stretch out on my quilt-covered bed, memories haunt me. I can't shut them off. I text my best friend Thorn, a high school freshman like me. Then, as I've done so many nights, I swing a leg, then the other, over my windowsill and slide onto the porch roof, careful to avoid the places that need repair. The noxious smell of the paper mill three miles away assaults my nose. It's stronger than usual tonight.

It's mid-February, and, while it's not cold in the Florida Panhandle, the air is a bit chilly now the sun's gone down. A breeze blows a wisp of thick, dark hair into my face. I brush it aside and stride to the roof's edge, jump, and front-flip midair. Landing in a crouch, I roll to break my fall. It's no problem for me. Just another bit of freerunning. And that's what I do best.

I pull my phone from my pocket and text: "Meet me at the playground."

My phone buzzes, and I read the one-word answer. "Now?"

"It's important."

Almost instantly, the phone vibrates again. "On my way."

I stick my phone in my pocket, then jog down the street to the elementary school playground where I first saw freerunning in action—a group of older boys racing around the playground, going over, instead of around, the benches and play equipment.

The combination of gymnastic and acrobatic moves, creative yet intentional, had intrigued me. Soon I was trying to copy them, laying claim to that same playground. Stairs with a center railing lead up to the school, high on a hill above the playground. I jog up those stairs, staying to the right of the railing. At the top, I turn and peer into the darkness below.

A lone streetlight casts a glow on the playground. The other lights were broken long ago and never replaced. The play area is a large asphalt square, surrounded by fields on two sides. The hill where I'm standing makes up the third side. A road runs beside the playground and dead ends into a rusty chain-link fence behind a convenience store on the fourth side. The store owners put up the fence to keep kids from going onto their property, but it's in bad shape and does little to keep anyone away.

How long before Thorn gets here? I need to talk to him, to tell him the news I received earlier that made my world tilt. I gaze around, but there's only the four netless basketball hoops perched on posts, like sentinels guarding the old-fashioned play equipment. No Thorn yet.

The images start to come, the same ones that have haunted me for years. A young girl celebrating her sixth birthday. Twirling round and round in a new pink party dress and white sandals with straps that wrap around her ankles. Feeling like a princess.

I know what's coming next, so I jump to my feet and race down the stairs, vaulting back and forth across the center railing until I reach the playground. Trying to escape the pictures playing in my mind, I cross the asphalt and run toward a bench, planting my hand on the back and bringing both legs over for a speed vault.

The swings, bars, slides, and merry-go-round in front of me are well-worn and a bit rusty, but they hold the memories of thousands of children over the years. This equipment is clustered around a newer wooden playset made up of ladders, bridges, slides, and climbing bars that work well for the jumps, flips, and vaults that make up freerunning.

The dim glow of the streetlight illuminates Thorn as he approaches the playground. He's wearing long cotton pajama bottoms, a black tank top, and high-top basketball shoes, same as me, but my shoes are black and white and held together with silver duct tape.

The slight chill of the night air doesn't bother us. We stay warm freerunning. I stride along the border of the playground near Thorn. He falls in beside me and matches his stride to mine. He has his own issues to deal with, so he gets it when I need to run away from the memories that haunt me. Most nights we run in silence in our own version of follow-the-leader.

Passing me, Thorn heads toward a brick wall meant to close off the corner of the playground housing the dumpster and storage shed. It doesn't accomplish that task but gives us a good wall for stunts. Planting his foot hip-high against the wall, Thorn pushes upward off the bricks and performs a perfect back flip. I follow, but back flips are tricky for me. I plant my foot wrong when I push off, sending me downward instead of into the air. I land hard on my bottom.

Thorn drops beside me. "Interesting move."

"Yeah, needs a little work."

"You forgot to drive your knee upward."

I snort. "Obviously."

My mood darkens as I remember why I wanted to talk to him. Thorn lifts an eyebrow. "What?"

"He called. Mom talked to him."

"Kia ..."

My heart lightens at Thorn's nickname for me. To everyone else, I'm Kiana Scott, but to Thorn, I'm just Kia. Like the car.

"He called," I repeat. "Just like that. Like he has a right." By saying the words aloud, I'm acknowledging it to myself. The *he* isn't my dad, because I don't know who my father is. It's the other he. The one who ruined me—Mom's father.

I jump up and take off, circling the playground with long, strong strides, trying unsuccessfully to slam the door of my mind on the thought of him. Thorn follows me as I weave in and out of the basketball poles, swinging myself in a wide arc on each pole.

I race to the horizontal bars, swing up, and sit. Thorn lands beside me, sweat glistening on his skin. Our arms touch, his white, mine light brown. Thorn calls me dusky.

He tilts his head to the side, studying me. "What does he want?"

I scoot to the edge of the bars and swing my legs back and forth. "Has cancer." I say it fast to cover the tremor in my voice. "Says he wants Mom's support."

"Really?" Thorn tightens his lips, then speaks again. "Her support?"

"So he says." I reach in my pocket and feel the Statue of Liberty souvenir coin my third-grade teacher gave me for getting a 100% on my geography test. I've carried it with me since. Prizes are rare in my world. I rub the coin between my thumb and first finger.

Thorn's eyes narrow. "He expects your mom to do what?"

"Don't know. But now, I'm thinking of what he did all over again." I release the coin and rub the back of my neck.

Thorn gives a quiet laugh. Not the kind that means something's funny ... the other kind. "Like you ever stopped. Like you even could."

I swing my legs harder. "I try."

He turns toward me. "You run."

I shrug one shoulder. "It's what I do best. Run."

Thorn's face is only inches from mine, his warm breath tickling my cheek. "Maybe it's time you face the issue."

If only it were that easy. If only bile didn't rise in my throat thinking about it. "It's too late. It can't be undone. I'll never be a normal teen. Normal was stolen from me."

Thorn looks thoughtful. He runs his hand backward through his closely clipped dark-blonde hair. What can he say? I'm right.

"True ..."

"But?"

"There's always hope."

"Hope for what?"

"A new ending. You can't change the beginning, but you don't have to let him write the ending too."

At Thorn's words, I feel a spark of some emotion I can't name. I don't know what to do or say, so I jump from the bars and cross the playground to the road home. Thorn is behind me as I jog down the street. Two dogs have tipped over a trashcan and are scavenging through the contents. The stench of rotted food invades my senses, making the inside of my nose burn. I speed up, and Thorn keeps pace. We race to my house where I grasp the cool metal porch post and pull myself up, hand over hand, my muscles taut.

I reach the roof. My fingertips grasp the edge. I pull myself up, ignoring the pain as rough shingles bite into my skin. Thorn is right behind me. We sit side by side next to my bedroom window, leaning against the house. My skin prickles from the cool aluminum siding. My tank top isn't warm enough now that we've stopped running, but I'm not ready to go inside yet.

The clouds part, and points of light blaze above us. Why does the night sky make me long for something I can't even name? I gaze upward and point. "There's Orion. See the three stars in a row? That's his belt."

I glance at Thorn. He's motionless, knees to his chest, arms wrapped loosely around them. His lips are slightly parted, and he gazes upward.

From down the street, a child's cry is followed by yelling and the crash of shattering glass, breaking the spell cast by the expanse of stars. Just another night on Willow Street, a place where people dump their junk curbside until the next pick-up day, so a constant assortment of old tires, appliances, and bathroom fixtures adorn the roadside the way trees and flowers do in other sections of town. A sigh escapes my lips. My surroundings are a reminder that my life has too much debris and not enough flowers.

Thorn turns to me, a question in his eyes.

I take a breath and blow it out slowly. "Why'd he have to call? Isn't it enough that I relive his abuse over and over in my dreams?"

I pull my knees to my chest and clutch them tightly until they start to cramp. I release my grip and stretch my legs. There's another tear in my shoe. I need more duct tape, my solution to most things in my life. But duct tape can't fix everything.

"Maybe he's got regrets," Thorn says.

I don't turn to face him, but I know he's watching me. I can feel it. I huff, air escaping from my nostrils. "Regrets for what he did to me? Not likely. Shouldn't make a difference to me anyway. I'm not six anymore."

"If it didn't make a difference, the memories wouldn't still haunt you."

I pull my legs to my chest and lean forward. "You know what it's like to hide something. To pretend it never happened. My grandfather. Your dad." I turn my head to look at him. "You and me? We both come from a hard place."

Thorn shifts sideways, looking directly at me. "Doesn't change the fact there's a plan for us. Someone bigger than us is orchestrating things."

Thorn's face is illuminated by the stars and a dim streetlight. I look into his shadowed blue eyes, searching my face. I open my mouth, trying to form an answer. This isn't the first time we've had this conversation.

"If there is a God, how could he sit back and watch what my grandfather did to me? What your dad did to you and your mom? What kind of God would let little kids get hurt?"

Thorn looks down and shakes his head. "I don't know the answer to that. But I know I trust him, look to him for courage, for the strength to do what it takes to make things change. Maybe it's time you claim the courage to do what you need to do."

I press my lips together, then exhale. "Like what? Have a chat with my grandfather? Tell him I forgive him for what he did? No thanks."

"No. Not that. But maybe you're meant to finally face it. Start writing your new ending."

I breathe in slowly through my nose and out my mouth. "Why now? I don't even know where to begin."

He turns his head to look at me. "Why not now? Don't let him win."

Heat rushes through me. Thorn doesn't get it. My grandfather has already won. "I can't talk about this more. I need to sleep."

I stand. Thorn looks up at me, but for now the conversation is over. I turn and slip through the open window into my room, then look back and watch as Thorn walks to the edge of the roof. He drops from view, and I hear a soft thud. His shadow disappears into the night.

Chapter Two

I wake before my alarm goes off and roll out of bed, landing on the cold floor. When I pull back the curtain, I'm greeted by a gloomy February morning. The house is quiet. Mom isn't up yet.

I search through the clean clothes piled on top of my dresser—the drawers have fallen apart again—and pull jeans and a soft black sweater from the heap. My comfort clothes let me blend in and stay under the radar of the mean girls at school. I'm not a coward, but I avoid trouble, which means not drawing attention to myself and not becoming the next target of bored rich kids.

The stairs creak as I creep down, not wanting to wake Mom. I go into the kitchen and turn on the coffee maker. She'll want at least one cup before she leaves for her job at the public health office. She doesn't love the job, but she doesn't hate it like she did most of her previous jobs. The work pays the bills—if only she sticks with it.

The refrigerator doesn't offer many choices, so I settle on blueberry yogurt. Mom joins me in the kitchen as I scrape the last miniscule blueberry from the bottom of the plastic container. She pours a cup of coffee and sits across from me at the table. She sips the brew, then wraps her hands around the brown ceramic mug and rubs her thumb up and down the handle. Her mouth opens, but no words come out.

Our eyes meet. Hers are filled with worry, but at least they're clear. She lowers her gaze and stares into her cup. I tense as her lips part, then close. "You know I've done my best by you." She glances up at me, then looks away. "My dad wasn't always the way he is now." She rubs her thumb harder against the mug handle, up and down, up and down. "He had his own plans for me." She pauses.

A stream of air escapes my lips. "Go on."

"Then I got pregnant right after graduation. He's never forgiven me for that."

"What's to forgive? You were seventeen. It was your life, not his."

"He was embarrassed. Then, when you were born, and I decided to keep you ..."

"He was embarrassed? By you being pregnant?"

"Not just that, but ..."

"But what?"

"Never mind. It doesn't matter."

"He was embarrassed by me, wasn't he? My color?"

"His generation saw things differently. He ..."

Before she can say more, I push back from the table, my chair scraping loudly. I toss my empty yogurt container in the trashcan, then turn to face Mom. "Why are you telling me this? It's past. What he thinks doesn't matter. I don't understand why you're letting him call."

Her lips tighten as she looks into her mug.

I cross my arms and stare at her. "What?"

"It's going to be more than phone calls. He's decided to come here."

My breathing quickens. "Here? What do you mean by here?"

She wraps shaking hands tightly around the mug. "He's moving back. He'll be staying in an assisted-living facility."

"What? Here?" I place my hand on the back of a chair to stop my world from spinning. I clench my jaw. He shouldn't still affect me. I'm stronger than this. Still, for almost a year, I lived a nightmare—one that didn't end when I opened my eyes in the morning. "Why didn't you tell him he's not welcome? Not after what he did."

"You have to believe I didn't know. He was different with me. He was more ... well, I was his princess. He was too ... close."

The words push out. "But he hurt me. He did things to me."

"I didn't know that until later, when my mom was real bad from cancer. I thought about leaving, but I had nowhere to go. She told me what she suspected. That it had happened before ..."

"He should have gone to jail. He made me feel ... dirty." My voice breaks. I don't like feeling vulnerable. I squash down those feelings and let the anger surface. "It shouldn't have happened!"

Mom sighs. "I thought you'd forgotten. You never mentioned it again. If it was bothering you, why didn't you tell me?"

"I was trying to forget, but I can't. Why didn't you ever report him?"

"At the time, I was afraid to. You might have had to go to court to testify against him. When you never brought it up again, I assumed you'd forgotten. You were so young, after all. I didn't want to make things worse for you by dredging it all up, so I just let it go. When my mom died, I found out she'd bought this house with money from her brother. She planned to fix it up as a rental to have retirement money of her own, but she found out she had cancer and never got around to it. She left me this house and a little money to help with expenses." She shrugs. "So, this is what we've got."

"Nothing wrong with it, Mom. We have a whole house for the two of us."

"With holes in the porch roof, leaky pipes, no air conditioning, and heat that only works when it wants to."

"It's fine. But your dad coming back to town isn't fine. I don't like it."

"It'll be okay. He sounded totally different on the phone. He's not the same man anymore. I think this will be a new start for us."

I try to take a deep breath, but there's no breath to be had. My stomach clenches, and yogurt refluxes into my mouth. I race toward the bathroom and reach the toilet as my breakfast comes back up. When my stomach's empty, I brush my teeth and splash cool water on my face.

I study my reflection in the mirror. Anxiety fills my deep brown eyes as I run my fingers through my hair, which is short on the sides and longer on top, to detangle it and fluff it until it's even. I've been told I'm pretty, but I don't notice any beauty, only light-brown skin, a broad nose, and full lips that tell me my dad, whoever he is, has African roots.

A glance at my watch alerts me—time to leave for school. Backpack in hand, I head out, looking back as I pull the front door open. Mom is watching me. She lowers her chin and drops her gaze. She needs me to say everything will be okay. But I won't. Any hope of that has been sucked out of me. I step outside, pulling the door shut behind me. Thorn is waiting curbside in his truck, and I don't want to be late.

South Bay High is in the rich section of our city, but the zoning lines put half of the poor section in the rich high school. The other half goes to high school in the mill district just over the bridge, a few miles from where Thorn and I live. The area is known as the mill district because of the paper mill, which spews its rancid smell across the city.

Thorn pulls into the student parking lot where rusted cars and dented pickup trucks are sandwiched between Mercedes-Benzes and BMWs, a reminder that everyone is rich or poor, not much in the middle. Thorn and I are definitely from the poor side.

In middle school, the rich and poor kids went to separate schools—a middle school in the poor section, a middle school in the rich side of town, and another in the mill district. Mill residents aren't as deprived as those in the poor section since many of them have jobs at the mill, but the houses are old, and there are as many bars as stores.

I climb from the truck, and Thorn falls in, walking just behind me. My skin prickles. I glance around, and my eyes catch movement. A man with snow-white hair stands along the far edge of the parking lot, barely visible, watching me. I gasp, and my steps falter. Thorn bumps into me.

"What?" he says.

"Someone over there." I tilt my head to gesture.

Thorn glances that way. "No one's there."

I turn and look. He's right. Nothing but a couple of trees and a row of shrubs. "I guess ... I guess this thing about my grandfather is getting to me." I force a laugh. "Now I'm imagining him hiding in the bushes."

Thorn studies my face. "That's who you thought you saw? Your grandfather?"

I shrug. "I'm fine. I just wish ..." I don't finish the sentence as we walk across the parking lot and into the school.

A crowd blocks the hallway, attention riveted on the announcement board. Three girls dressed in low-cut jeans and form-fitting T-shirts stand in a tight clique, chattering excitedly. All three have long hair parted on the side, identical except for their hair color. One has light-brown hair with highlights, one has reddish-blonde hair that cascades down her back in waves, and one has straight, dark-brown hair with a tint of purple. Last time I saw her, her hair was turquoise. Leila, Zoey, and Kendra. You never see one alone. They are a trio bonded by prestige and power.

Thorn edges forward. I raise an eyebrow at him, silently asking him what's going on. He shrugs and pushes his way to the announcement board. A minute later he makes his way back to me. He lifts his chin and grins. "New track coach—Terrence Jones."

I'm missing something. "Who's that?"

"Who's that? Really? You didn't watch *Running Free: The Amazon Tour* last fall?"

Hands on my hips, I tilt my head and look at Thorn. "That reality show where the contestants had to run like a hundred miles through the Amazon? You know I don't watch reality shows."

Thorn nods. "But you watched it with me the first week when they introduced the competitors and showed their families. It came on when we were working on science homework together. Terrence Jones was the one who was from Miami. The African-American one."

"And ..."

"And he was the winner. He finished strong while the others barely dragged across the finish line. He was smiling while they all looked defeated and were complaining about everything from the weather to the insects and the river."

"And?"

Thorn grins. "He's a freerunner like us. That's what gave him an edge over the others. His freerunning skills helped him handle the challenges of the Amazon."

I cross my arms over my chest and stare at Thorn. "And he's

going to coach here? Are you sure it's the same guy?"

"Think so. They just hired him. With Coach Cleary having a heart attack during Christmas vacation, no one knew for sure what was going to happen with track."

"So he's the new head coach? Wasn't there already an assistant coach?"

Thorn shrugs. "There are two assistants—one for the boys, and one for the girls—but it sounds like they are bringing him in as head coach."

I give a dry laugh. "You'd think with all the publicity from the show, he'd get a job doing something more prestigious than coaching here."

Thorn shrugs.

Leila, Zoey, and Kendra are standing next to us now, listening. Like it's any of their business what Thorn and I are saying. They scrutinize me from my thick, dark-brown hair down to my duct-taped high tops. Leila, the blonde, steps toward me, rose-tinted lips curled. "South Bay's girls' track team did send runners to state last year." As if she had something to do with it. She and her sidekicks are freshmen, too. "And besides, he went to high school here before he moved to Miami, in case you didn't know. He's our own hometown hero. It makes perfect sense he'd come back."

I shrug. "So?"

She smirks. "Well, we three are going to be on the team, of course." She looks down at my shoes and wrinkles her nose. "But I guess that's not an option for you."

Zoey gives a phony laugh. "I don't think she can afford enough duct tape to make those shoes last a lap, much less a whole meet."

My hands clench into fist. I open my mouth, but Thorn takes my arm and pulls me away. "Come on. Let's get to class."

I turn my back on the trio and follow Thorn. He turns to look at me. "You could do it, you know."

I look at Thorn. "What?"

"Make the track team. Probably run and jump circles around those girls."

"Yeah. In my fancy track shoes." I snort. "I have more to worry about than Terrence Jones, hometown hero, and girls' track."

As class period after class period drags by, the questions in my head drown out the teachers' voices. Why does my grandfather have to come here? What will it mean for me?

Six o'clock and Mom isn't home yet. I open the refrigerator and look for something to eat. Nothing. I open the freezer and take out a packaged dinner. I slit the wrapper as instructed on the back of the box and microwave it. The house fills with the smell of a home-cooked meal—or as close to a home-cooked meal as happens in this house.

After I'm done eating, I take my backpack to the couch and pull out my algebra book. Notebook in front of me and pencil in hand, I try to work the first problem, but the numbers don't make sense. I shut the book, lean my head against the back of the couch and close my eyes. What would it be like to be on the track team? I'm a good jumper. I have to be to make the different vaults that are part of freerunning. But that's different from doing hurdles or the high jump in a competition.

Freerunning uses jumps, vaults, flips, anything you feel like doing. It's more like an attitude or a lifestyle. You have to be strong and flexible. Nerves of steel help too. But unlike track, there are no rules. And people aren't watching, at least not for those of us who run at night.

I drop my algebra book and my binder into my backpack. I have all weekend to do the math homework. Thoughts pound in my head, and I need to run to clear my mind.

Mom's probably drinking with friends. Who knows when she'll get home. But it's already dark out, so I turn on the outside light in case she arrives before me, then jog to the school.

The playground is empty, ready to be my personal arena. There are fancy gyms for freerunning—or parkour which is similar—but you don't have to have a gym. The obstacles on the school playground provide ample chance to work my skills.

I jog slowly, letting my muscles warm up. A shadow dashes to the large wooden play set in the middle of the playground. I watch Thorn's silhouette as he puts his palms flat on the top of a wooden beam, tucks his knees, then brings them through his arms for a kong vault. He easily clears the beam. His fluid motion makes freerunning look like a dance.

I watch as he dominates the playground. He runs up the stair rail to the top of the hill and back flips from the rail, following with front and side flips down the hill, then runs back up the stairs. He jumps window ledge to window ledge until he lands on the roof of the lowest part of the school building. Then he throws himself backward off the roof and does a series of flips midair. I catch my breath, exhaling as he lands gracefully on his feet.

The lone unbroken streetlight illuminates the brick wall by the dumpster as he jumps up and hits the wall, spinning his body over his hands and landing on the balls of his feet. Every move seems effortless and orchestrated, yet it's simply Thorn doing what he does.

He circles the playground more slowly. I drop into place behind him as he runs toward the wall, then executes a beautiful climb up. Imitating him, but without his skill or fluidity, I grab the wall, knuckles at the edge. My legs push against the roughness of the barrier, and I press down with my arms, joining Thorn at the top of the wall.

Thorn turns to me. "I was serious earlier. You could easily make the track team. Why don't you try out?"

I look at him. "Really? Track?"

"Sure. Why not?"

"Why don't you? You ran track in middle school."

He shrugs. "I don't have time with homework and my job. Things get busy for my grandfather's landscape business in the spring. He needs my help, and I need gas money for my truck."

I nod. I understand. I love the familiar rumble of his truck engine that fills the air before his rusty Ford pulls to the curb when he picks me up for school. At fifteen, Thorn only has a learner's permit, but no one pays attention to things like that in our neighborhood.

Thorn is watching me, waiting. I swing my legs back and forth, hitting my heels against the wall. I shrug. "Why not? But if I do, you do. Your grandfather would understand. You could help after practice. No promises I'll make the team, though."

"Of course you will. You're a strong runner and jumper."

"Is there a jump-over-the-park-bench event? Or cat-climb event? I don't have much experience with anything else."

"You could do hurdles. High jump. Long jump. I ran the 1600-meter and 4 by 800 relay in middle school." Thorn looks at my high tops, then his own. "Those girls were right about the shoes, though. No matter what events we do, we'll have to get running shoes. Something with good tread. Track cleats would be better, but those are too expensive."

Heat creeps up my neck. "How are we supposed to get new shoes?"

I study my high tops. I like them. They were worn out six months ago, but they still fit, and I feel comfortable in them. Still, sometimes I have trouble with freerunning moves requiring traction, like wall climbs, since the tread is long worn away.

"I have money saved from my job. It doesn't all go into the gas tank. Besides, the shoe store by the mall always has a buy-one-get-one-half-price sale. If I show my school ID, I get another ten percent off."

Thorn is offering me a favor, but it doesn't feel right. I reach in my pocket and wrap my hand around my Statue of Liberty souvenir coin, rubbing it between my thumb and first finger. I want to say no, but I need the shoes. Neither of us gets much new stuff. And in our neighborhood, no one gets to be picky about brands or keeping up with styles. No way is Mom going to get me new shoes.

I swallow. "Okay. Thanks." I hesitate. "I'll pay you back. When I can."

Thorn shrugs. "I'm not worried."

We flip from the wall and start walking down the road toward home. My thoughts are a tangled mess.

Thorn can tell. "What are you thinking?"

I hesitate. "Thinking about too much. My grandfather, of course, but now I'm thinking about track too. Like maybe track will open some doors for me. Maybe this is my shot at normal."

Thorn laughs. "Normal is overrated."

I nod. "Yeah, but track's a regular activity. Like other girls do. But part of me is saying it's a big mistake. I'll always be who I am whether I'm on a team or not." I sigh. "Besides, I can't even afford to buy my own running shoes."

"I said I'd take care of it for you."

"Feels wrong."

"Because I want to help you?"

I blow out a quick burst of air. "Doesn't happen in our world."

He gives a dry laugh. "Because you don't let it happen."

I look sideways at him. "We're not talking about shoes anymore, are we?"

He doesn't answer.

I stop walking. "Is this another pep talk about there being a God who has a plan? Because I'm not seeing it. All I'm seeing is the man who abused me is walking back into my life. You say it's time to move on, but I don't know how to do that. How am I supposed to face him?"

"Don't face him. Face what he did. Talk to someone who knows how to help people with this kind of thing."

I look down and shake my head. It's all too much. I start racing toward home, leaving Thorn behind.

"Hey, wait up." His footsteps are gaining on me, and he falls into place beside me, matching his steps to my own. He opens his mouth but closes it without saying anything.

"What?" I ask, slowing to a walk.

"Ever wonder if your dad was a runner?" he asks.

I look sideways at him. "That's random."

He shrugs. "You're fast, and your mom doesn't seem like a runner to me."

"Oh, she runs all right," I say. "Every time there's a problem, she runs to the nearest bar. But my father? I've never given him much thought. Guess I assumed he was a loser."

"You never wondered what you inherited from him?"

"My color obviously. Beyond that, who knows?"

Thorn is silent. We walk another half block before he speaks. "I wonder about it. About what combination of my parents made me who I am."

"Does it matter?" I ask.

"Maybe."

Silence hangs heavy. I wait.

Thorn starts to speak in the slow way he has when he's processing something aloud. "My dad has always had temper problems. Everything blew up the night Mom tried to talk to him about how he was treating me. They were outside, and Dad hit her so hard she fell and hit her head on the curb. Died later in the hospital. What if whatever made my dad kill my mom is in me too? If it is, can I overcome it? Or will it always be part of me?"

"Thorn ..."

"No. Really ..." he interrupts. "What if that's the way it is? What if whatever your parents are is what you'll become? Whether it's good or bad?"

I stop, face him, and place my hand on his arm. "You're the best person I know. You care about everyone." I give him a playful punch in the arm. "You're also the most stubborn person in the world at times."

He snorts. "Me stubborn? Look who's talking." He turns serious again. "I wonder about my dad and me sometimes."

"Tomorrow is your Saturday to visit him at the prison, isn't it? You worried about it?"

Thorn shrugs and resumes walking. A few minutes later, we're at my house. I want to say something both comforting and profound, but nothing comes to mind. I sigh. "Good luck tomorrow. Text me if you want. If you have minutes left." Most kids have iPhones or at least smart phones, but Thorn and I make do with the old kind that use minute cards you buy each month.

He nods, turns, and walks toward his house four blocks away. When I enter the house, I hear the shower running. I lock the back door, turn out the lights, and head upstairs. I test myself to see if I can make it without hitting the squeaky spots—step to the right on the second step and to the left on the sixth step. Skip the seventh step altogether. I almost make it when I forget about the next to the top step and it lets out an aching groan.

The water stops, and Mom calls out, "Kiana?"

"Going to bed, Mom. Long day."

"Okay, goodnight."

I let out a slow stream of air, forcing myself to relax. I need to sleep. I'm not good at change, and the changes ahead are going to take all my energy.

Chapter Three

On Monday morning, a crowd is once again gathered around the announcement board. I inch my way forward until I can read the notice, a reminder that track tryouts will be after school today for the boys and Wednesday for the girls. Thorn will be trying out, though he's not sure he can stay on the team because of work.

After school, I join the spectators to watch the boys' track tryouts. Thorn is wearing his new shoes. When he told his grandparents he was planning to buy shoes for himself and me, his grandfather insisted on paying for them. He bought nice ones too, and even got them in blue and gold to match our track uniforms. Thorn brought the shoes over yesterday afternoon, and we went for a jog to start breaking them in.

When I arrive, a man is pacing up and down in front of the bleachers. I recognize him from that reality TV episode I watched with Thorn. The new track coach, Terrence Jones, is around six feet tall, lean, and muscular. His tightly curled black hair is cut short. His shirt sleeves pull tight around his biceps, the white material in contrast to his brown skin.

I can't hear what he's saying, but I can guess by his gestures. He holds up his clipboard and points at the track. Several boys take a lane. He blows a whistle, and the guys take off. Four laps around. By my watch, the first runner comes in at 5:54.03. Impressive, but Thorn isn't much behind.

One event follows another—sprints, relays, hurdles, high jump, long jump, triple jump, pole vault, and other field events. The coach is narrowing down the best at each event. Finally, sweat-drenched, looking exhausted but exhilarated, Thorn joins me. He cracks the lid on a sports drink from the team cooler and takes a long swallow. He looks at me and grins. "Now you know what kind of fun you're in for on Wednesday."

Wednesday afternoon comes too soon, and my stomach is fluttering. I force myself to take calming breaths as I walk to the locker room to change into my PE shorts. It's either that or try out in the sleep pants I often wear to freerun. I don't think that would be appropriate. Thorn made the boys' team. Now I need to make the girls' team.

There's already a crowd of girls waiting by the track as I sign my name on a clipboard. I'm number 34, and a long line of girls are behind me, waiting to sign in. Who knew track was this popular? I find a place to sit on the bleachers. Thorn is outside the fence with a crowd of guys who are there out of curiosity or to watch their girlfriends try out.

Almost ten minutes later, Terrence Jones walks in and picks up the clipboard. A female coach walks up to him. Her skin is the color of milk chocolate, and her hair is short like a boy's. She's more muscular than most women. While Coach Jones has an easy grin on his face, she's glowering. Without the scowl, she'd be pretty. I know she's Cassandra Clark, the assistant coach for girls' cross country and track. She's in last year's team photo in the trophy case in the school's front hall.

Coach Jones glances across the group of girls seated on the bleachers. He clasps his hands behind him and makes eye contact with several of us. "Welcome to the girl's track tryouts." He looks down at the clipboard. "According to this list, there are ninety-eight of you here to try out. That must be a record."

His deep voice holds a hint of humor. He offers a half smile, his mouth raised on one side. "We are going to work hard this year, so unless you are here because you love running so much that you're willing to give it your best—without complaining—even when you're hot and tired and your muscles are cramping—you might want to find another activity."

The sound of girls whispering spreads across the bleachers, but no one gets up to leave. He slowly scans the sea of faces in front of him, looking at each of us. A few giggle and nudge each other.

Coach Jones raises his eyebrows. "No? You're all here to run hard and sweat?" He tightens his lips and then breaks into a grin. "Okay, then. Let's get started. Coach Clark and I will give each of you a fair chance, but you're not going to make the team unless you earn it. If we had more time, we'd spend a couple of weeks training together and seeing what each of you is capable of, but since we are getting a late start, you only have today to show us what you can do."

Coach Clark stands in front of us, arms crossed. She looks across the bleachers. Her eyes focus on me, like she's studying me. I look into her eyes, refusing to look away. Her eyes narrow. I get a heavy feeling in my stomach. Have I done something wrong? She turns her gaze away, and I let out a breath. What was that all about?

Coach Clark scowls. "Unlike Coach Jones, I'm not amused so many of you showed up for tryouts." There's a lilt to her voice. Jamaican, maybe? Jamaican tinged with anger. "Most of you girls don't look like you can make it around the track, much less do it at a run. So, if you're just here to meet our celebrity coach, take a photo on your phone and leave. If you can't run fast and jump high and long, you're no use to us."

She glances my way again. Is she talking to me? I can run and jump. Why would she single me out?

Coach Jones chuckles. "That might be a bit harsh, but we do need everyone on the team to be able to do those things with some practice." He points to the track. "One lap of the track is 400 meters or about a quarter of a mile. We're going to start with a 1600-meter run ... four laps."

Coach Clark glowers at him, but he doesn't seem to notice and continues talking. "When I call your name, find a spot on the track. Due to the large number of you here, we'll be running more than the usual eight at a time." He calls out names, and those girls walk onto the track and find a spot. I'm in the third group to run. While I'm not first, I'm also not last.

The times are slow, fast, and everything in between. The slowest one is 18:52. She barely makes the 1600. The fastest is Michaela Dugin, a senior who's been on the team all through high school. She comes in at 6:13.01.

After all ninety-eight girls have run, Coach Jones walks to the front and faces us. "Some of you are clearly runners, and some of you are going to have to push a lot harder if you want a place on the team. Now that you're warmed up, we're going to get down to business. At any time, you can simply cross your name off the list and leave. It's no shame. God has gifted each of us differently."

Coach Jones is obviously an athlete, but does he really think God gave him that? Does God pass out different talents to different people? If he's right, there are certainly some girls here who were passed over for the running gift.

Coach Jones glances across the bleachers one more time. "While half of you are running, Coach Clark will be taking the other half to do high jump and long jump. Let's have numbers one through forty-five go with Coach Clark. The rest of you get ready to run sprints and relays."

I stand and follow the procession of girls headed to the high jump pit. Coach Clark faces us. "Most of you are wasting my time, but our new head coach says everyone gets a chance. Sasha will show you high jump form, then it's your turn."

We sit in the grass as Sasha takes her place. She sprints toward the high jump pole, curving in as she nears it, then turning her body and driving her knee up to go over it backward. She makes it look simple. I'm guessing it's not.

"We're starting at three feet. Line up and let's go." Coach Clark stands next to the bar, clipboard in hand. "One miss and you're out. Then you go sit by the long jump pit and wait for your turn there."

About a third of the girls miss the very first jump. I sprint at the bar, then curve in like a J. I drive my knee up and arch my back, clearing the bar, though not gracefully. I land on the thick blue mat on the other side and run my hand over the smooth surface. The springiness of the mat is different from the dirt and concrete I'm used to when I freerun.

Coach inches the bar up. More girls knock the bar from the poles. Coach's brows furrow a little more with each miss. Her grip tightens on her pen as she writes on her clipboard. I clench and unclench my fists as I wait for each turn, relaxing as I make the second round and then the third. Finally, only Sasha James and I are left. My jumps aren't graceful like hers, but I'm clearing the bar. I miss at 5-4. Sasha misses at 5-6.

Coach Clark looks my way. "You do high jump in middle school?"

I shake my head. "No, but I freerun. That uses a lot of jumping."

She forces air through her nose, and her nostrils widen. She looks at her clipboard. "Your name is Kiana Scott?"

"Yes," I answer.

She nods as though confirming something, then turns away.

I try to push aside the feeling that something is wrong as I take my place by the long jump pit, trailing my fingers through the sand. Someone nudges me with her foot. I glance back. Zoey smirks. "Show off much?"

"What?"

"You heard me. 'Oh, I'm so good at this because I freerun,'" she says in a singsong voice. "You think that'll get you in with the new coach? Because he freeruns too? I'm sure you know that from the show. Probably couldn't wait to meet him, huh?"

I turn back to the pit, ignoring her. She nudges me with her foot again, and while I'm tempted to turn around and punch her, I slide forward out of her reach instead.

Coach Clark walks to the long jump pit, hands Sasha the end of a tape measure, and walks backward down the pit. She stops and draws a line, then glances around. "Ten feet. If you can't jump that far, go over to the track."

A freshman who sits by me in math raises her hand. She's friendly but doesn't appear athletic. Coach nods at the girl, annoyance evident in her expression. "Isn't ten feet kind of far?" the girl asks.

"I jumped eighteen feet, four inches my senior year of high school. Farther in college. You can't do it? Go home and play some video games." Coach Clark's accent grows stronger as her agitation increases.

The girl draws into herself. Coach Clark turns her back, stands on the takeoff board, and walks straight back several yards. "Line up here. Michaela will go first and show you how it's done."

Michaela takes off while Coach narrates. "Start a sprint and drive toward the pit. Step on the board—try for the same spot every time—then jump."

Michaela launches from the board and looks like she's running through the air. She'd make a great freerunner. She hits the sand several feet past the ten-foot mark.

When my turn comes, I focus on the ten-foot line in the pit, sprint until I hit the board, and pretend I'm making a freerun jump. I clear the line with several feet to spare, landing solidly in the sand on both feet. It was weak, but now that I have the feel, I'll do better.

Coach gives us three jumps and writes down our longest one. Mine is 15-06, not bad for a first try. Freerunning has paid off for me in the jumps.

Our group jogs to the track to trade places with the group there. The mood quickly lightens as Coach Jones has us run our sprints, infusing his instructions with humor.

When both groups are done and assembled in the bleachers, Coach Jones addresses us. "I'll be looking at your running times and your high jump and long jump distances to decide who makes the team." He stops and glances across the bleachers. "Thank you all for coming out, and if your name is listed on the board tomorrow morning, be here after school on Monday, ready to work." He dismisses us with a wave as he turns and walks away.

I head over to find Thorn, confident that I did good. I just hope it was good enough.

The next morning, Thorn pulls into the school parking lot five minutes before the bell. Again, a crowd has gathered around the bulletin board. I can't get close enough to read the list, but it's only one page. It doesn't take long for each girl to find her name—or discover it's not on the list.

I make my way to the board, slipping between the other girls. I quickly realize the names are listed by the finish times on the 1600. Michaela Dugin is the first name on the list. No surprise there. Sasha James is second. I scan down the list until I see my name, Kiana Scott. I'm number six. Not bad. Kendra is listed right under me. She's faster than I thought. Maybe she didn't try out only to meet Terrence Jones. I quickly look down the list for Leila and Zoey. They are the last two names. Still, they made it. Did I misjudge them? Do they really want to be track stars?

The rest of the day, I try to concentrate on my classes, but my mind keeps returning to track. For the first time ever, I'm on a team. One part of me can't wait to start practices. The other part wonders if I've made a mistake. What do I know about track? Will being on the team be a new start for me—a way to regain what my grandfather took? Maybe. I wish practice started today, not Monday.

After school, Thorn pulls up in front of my house, parking behind an unfamiliar silver convertible. "Whose car is that?"

I shrug. "Probably someone visiting one of the neighbors. No one around here drives an expensive sports car."

Thorn's truck engine rumbles in a familiar way as he puts the truck in park and turns to me. "You think your mom will be happy you're on the team?"

I shrug. "I don't think she paid much attention when I told her about try-outs. She just signed the permission slip and handed it back."

I step from the truck and jog to the house. Maybe she will be proud. After all, it's the first team I've ever been on. I pause outside the door. I hear loud voices, and I strain to hear.

"Melonie, please. Just a few days. That's all I'm asking. Just until I'm able to work something out. Think of all I did for you before you got this house."

My breath catches. It can't be! I ease the back door open and slip inside. My mother is standing face-to-face with a man with snow-white hair. All the air seems sucked from the room as I step far enough into the room to catch sight of his face, the face from my nightmares. As I fight to restore air to my lungs, another horrible realization hits me. If my grandfather is here in my neighborhood, then maybe I hadn't imagined him watching me from the bushes at school. But why, after almost ten years, would he bother?

Chapter Four

I suck in air, and they both turn to look at me. Although only in his early sixties, my grandfather's hair is white. The snow-colored hair, blue eyes, and wide smile give him the friendly façade of a mall Santa. But I know the truth. I meet his eyes, and my stomach roils.

"Kiana, how good to see you again." His words are like silk.

The room feels hot, and my head is spinning. I steady myself with a hand on the back of a chair and turn to my mother with unspoken questions.

I open my mouth, then close it. I swallow. "Why didn't you tell me he was coming here?"

Mom turns to me. "I didn't know. He came early to surprise us."

I turn to my grandfather. "How long have you been in town?"

He looks at me. There's something unreadable in his eyes. "I just got here. I've had a long drive, and I'm tired. This isn't the welcome I expected. My own daughter arguing about me staying with her. I helped your mom out when she needed it. Now I need her help."

"After what you did?"

A hurt look crosses my grandfather's face. "Why bring up past misunderstandings?"

The room suddenly feels too hot. "Misunderstandings? Is that what you call it?"

I turn to Mom.

She won't meet my eyes. "He needs a place to stay. Just for a few days."

"You aren't seriously going to let him stay here?" Panic fills my voice. I clench my fists to stop my hands from shaking.

"Just until he gets settled and arranges housing."

"I thought he was going to be in an assisted-living facility?"

My grandfather smiles. "The accommodations aren't ready yet."

"What about a hotel?" I demand.

"Certainly you don't begrudge me housing, Kiana?"

I open my mouth to speak, but no words come out.

Mom looks at me with pleading in her eyes. "It will be okay. I'll make sure it's okay. He doesn't have the money for a hotel right now. He'll stay in my room, and I'll sleep in the spare room until things get worked out."

"He'll stay in your room while you sleep on that ratty couch in the junk room?"

My grandfather speaks. "It'll be nice to get reacquainted now that you're older, Kiana." He gives me a wide smile, but his eyes are another story. A shudder runs through me.

A vision starts to form. A small girl in a pink dress twirling to make the bottom of the dress billow. I close my mind to the memories that threaten to overwhelm me. I turn and race toward the door, looking back at Mom. "I'll be staying with Thorn and his grandparents until he's gone."

I leave the house, wrapping my arms across my chest to still the shaking. I force myself to take a deep breath, then blow it out slowly.

I pull out my phone and text Thorn. Then I turn and run. I hit the schoolyard at a sprint, not slowing as I near a bench. I position my left hand on the back of it, the rough wood biting into my hand as I bring my body up and clear the bench with a side vault. I sprint toward the playset in the center of the playground, bend toward the low balance beam, and do a handstand on it. My shoulder muscles are taut as I launch into a series of front walkovers, a gymnastics move Thorn taught me. Finally, I flip off the other end, my feet making solid contact with the old asphalt.

Racing toward the wall, I hit it high, my fingers gripping the rough concrete as I pull up and sit on the top. I look around. Large rolls of fencing are piled at the end of the playground near the basketball hoops. They weren't there before. They're fencing the playground! Where will we freerun? There's another park nearby, but it's not as good, and it's not always safe because it's a known hangout for teens smoking marijuana. I push a strong stream of air between my lips. Maybe I'm borrowing trouble. Maybe it won't be locked after hours. Who am I kidding? Of course, it will be.

Not even six o' clock yet, and it's already dark, one of the drawbacks of being on Central Time. I spot movement at the edge of the playground. Thorn is a shadow in the falling darkness. He hits the wall at a run and easily makes it to the top to sit by me.

I turn to him. "He's here. That fancy silver car was his." I hate the way my voice quivers when I say it.

Thorn's eyes widen. "He's here right now? In your house?"

I nod. "He and Mom were arguing about him staying with us."

"Your mom didn't tell you?"

"Said she didn't know. He wanted to surprise us."

"I bet it was a surprise. So, is she letting him stay with you?"

I kick my heels against the wall. "In her room while she sleeps in the junk room. Says it's just for a few days till he gets finances worked out. He played the 'I helped you when you needed it, so now you need to help me' card. Said he wants us to be a family now."

"What about protecting you? Keeping him away from you?"

"Mom says she'll make sure I'm okay. But I told her I was staying with you and your grandparents until he's gone. You think that'll be okay?"

Thorn gave a dry laugh. "Yeah. But you'd probably be safe anyway. Guys like him—they like them young. You're too old."

"That's totally sick."

Thorn nods. "Sick, but true."

Thorn's fingers touch mine. We sit in silence, not needing words to know how the other feels.

I stand and front flip to the dumpster and then to the ground before sprinting across the playground. Thorn is right behind me. I slow and point out the fencing.

He shakes his head. "Bad news for us."

I nod. My gut had already confirmed that for me. I race toward the bench and clear it with a side vault, adding a front handspring before coming to a stop. "What will we do?"

Thorn shakes his head again. "Find a new place. What else can we do?" He sprints toward the steps, lands on the center railing, runs it to the top, and front flips off. I follow. He remounts the rail, does a handstand to a backbend position and back to a standing position, repeating the movements faster and faster. I follow, running the railing behind him.

Thorn jogs across the playground to the road home. I fall in place beside him as we head to his grandparents' house. No way am I going near my house as long as my grandfather is there. We enter the front door, and his grandparents look away from the game show they're watching. Thorn makes eye contact with his grandmother. "Her grandfather is here. Okay if she stays with us until he's moved out?"

His grandmother agrees. Thorn has probably told her at least a little about my grandfather. Besides, I've stayed overnight before, once for a whole week when my mom was in the hospital.

"You'll call her mom and make it okay?" Thorn confirms.

"Certainly." She lifts the receiver from the phone mounted on the wall. My number is written on a scrap of paper tucked under the edge.

Thorn hands me a pile of DVDs. "You pick the movie, and I'll make the popcorn."

I blink back tears. Funny how family can feel like strangers and friends can become family.

I wake on the couch, still wearing my clothes from yesterday, an afghan knitted in shades of blue over me, a pillow under my head. Thorn is asleep in the recliner, a faded red-checked blanket over him. He's wearing yesterday's school clothes too. I kept him up too late talking about my grandfather.

Thorn opens his eyes and sits up. "You okay?"

"Okay as I can be with my grandfather here. What am I going to do? Even once he moves out of the house, he'll still be in town."

"Stay strong. That's all you can do. You're not a child anymore. He can't hurt you."

My head pounds. I rub the back of my neck. "Not physically.

But the way he looked at me ...”

Thorn showers while I eat the scrambled eggs his grandmother serves me. Minutes later he joins me, hair still wet.

He checks his watch as he forks eggs into his mouth. “We have to get to school. We’ll stop at your house so you can change clothes, then pick up the rest of your stuff after school.”

We ride in silence the few blocks to my house. Thorn pulls to the curb. I turn to him. “You want to wait in the truck? I’ll shower and change quickly.”

Thorn stares straight ahead for a minute, then shakes his head. “No. If he’s in there, I want to be with you.”

I kick at the ground. “Don’t let his looks fool you. He could play Santa Claus, but on the inside, he’s Satan.” I open the truck door and climb out. “Maybe he’ll still be in bed.”

He’s not. He’s drinking coffee at the table. Like he belongs. I refuse to make eye contact with him.

Mom looks up. “Good morning Kiana ... Thorn.”

“Good morning,” Thorn replies, but he’s sizing up my grandfather.

My grandfather looks briefly at Thorn, lifts his coffee mug, and takes a sip.

I jog up the stairs, grab clean clothes from the pile on my dresser, and go into the bathroom, shutting the door firmly before locking it. I close my eyes as warm water cascades over me, but memories flood my mind. My skin prickles, and I scrub to erase the sensation. When I go back downstairs, Thorn is sitting on the couch. He stands as I enter the room, and we walk back through the kitchen. Mom is still at the table with her father. She looks at me expectantly as I enter. I want to leave without saying a word, but I don’t. Ignoring my grandfather, I say, “Bye, Mom.”

My grandfather sets his cup on his saucer with a bang. “That’s all you have to say?”

“What else do you think I should say?”

“You could try, ‘Good morning, Grandfather’.”

I swallow the acid rising in my throat along with the words I ache to spew at him.

Thorn steps forward and takes my elbow. “We need to go now,

or we'll be late." He leads me out the door.

After school, I meet up with Thorn in the parking lot. As his truck sputters to life, he states, "I need to gas up the truck for the weekend. Want to ride along? Or we can stop at your house first."

I shake my head. "No, thanks. My grandfather is probably there."

Thorn heads toward the mill district. "I found a new gas station over here. Almost ten cents cheaper."

We cross the bridge and start up the hill. The smell from the paper mill, like boiled eggs gone bad a month ago, assaults my nose.

A cat is sunning itself on the front porch of what was once a nice house, but now the porch sags and screens hang from the windows. Three boys kick a soccer ball in the front yard. In contrast, the house next to it looks newly painted, a mint-green with white trim around the windows. A rose bush climbs a trellis at the side of the house. As we head up the hill toward the mill, we pass a small family-owned hardware store. Wheelbarrows are lined up along the front in a neat row. Two men, standing next to a soda machine, look toward us and wave as Thorn's truck rambles by. Seems funny to see strangers waving, but I give a small wave in return.

Thorn stops for the light at the intersection nearest the mill. Several eighteen-wheelers, loaded with long pine logs, are waiting in a turn lane to enter the gate to the mill. A train is stopped on the tracks that run along the property, but it's far enough back that the gates aren't down. Colorful graffiti adorns the doors of the boxcars.

"That's some pretty amazing artwork," Thorn observes.

"How do they make such elaborate words on the cars? And how do they have time?"

Thorn studies the boxcars. "The train must be stopped at night—or no one pays much attention to kids painting on the side of a train."

"Too bad they can't use that talent to fix up some of these

buildings. They could do murals on the sides of these factories."

"The graffiti might not have been done in our town. Kids in any of the towns the train stops in could have done the artwork."

"True," I acknowledge.

The truck rattles across the train tracks. As Thorn pulls into a gas station. I glance across the street. A large brick church is across from the gas station. The church lawn is mowed and edged, and the green bushes are neatly trimmed. A van pulls up in front of the large glass doors, and children climb out. One little girl, no more than five or six, maybe even younger, jumps from the van and skips toward a playground surrounded by a high chain link fence. A lady, holding a clipboard, stands in the open gate. Turning back toward the van, the little girl grins and waves.

I turn to Thorn. "Look at that little girl. She looks a lot like I did at that age. Same light-brown skin and dark hair."

Thorn smiles. "She's a cutie."

"It looks busy over there. Wonder what's going on?"

"That's Mill District City Church," Thorn explains. "It always has a lot going on—programs for the little kids during the day and bigger kids after school. They're known for their community programs. I played there once on a peewee basketball league."

"Really! Who took you? Your dad? Or were you living with your grandparents by then?"

Thorn frowns.

"Sorry. I shouldn't have asked. Not my business."

Thorn shakes his head. "No. My dad took me. It was before ... my mom's death. They handed out a flyer at school that told about the program, and my dad thought it would be a good idea to get me in sports. Especially since it was free. It's just—"

I wait. Thorn clutches the steering wheel. "My father has never had any use for God. But last week when I visited, he said he found God. Said he's a new person. Wants a new start." Thorn's words rush together, but I understand them.

"But isn't that what you want? For your dad to change?"

Thorn hesitates. "I do. But I guess I wonder if this is for real. I mean, I know God can change people, but hearing Dad talk about God is ... well, different. He even wrote to me. Got it in the mail yesterday, so he had to have written it the same day I was there or the next."

I wait. I want to know what his dad said in the letter, but I want Thorn to volunteer the information. Instead, he climbs out and goes inside to pay for his gas. After he has pumped the gas, he climbs back into the truck and continues the conversation as though there was no break. "Said he's sorry. He has regrets. Wishes he could go back and do it all over. Stuff like that."

"But you don't think he means it?"

Thorn shrugs. "Even if I did, I don't know what to do with it."

He stops talking. I wait. He's trying to process things. Put them into words. Thorn shakes his head and speaks in a low voice. "Doesn't matter whether he has regrets or not. It doesn't change anything. I might be able to forgive him, but he'll still be in prison, and I'll still be living with my grandparents."

He's right. The hurt can't be undone, but would it feel different knowing the person who hurt you had regrets?

"I like your grandparents. I'd take them over my grandfather any day."

Thorn nods. "Yeah, they're good to me, and their faith has given me a strong foundation. But it's not the same as having parents."

I start to answer, but a silver car at the end pump catches my eye. "That looks like my grandfather's car."

I've no sooner said it than my grandfather walks out of the gas station, holding a Styrofoam cup with the gas station's logo on it. He pauses and looks across the street.

Thorn turns to look. "What's he looking at?"

I follow my grandfather's gaze. He's looking at the little girl who had caught my eye. She's on the playground now, and the gate is closed, but the children are still visible from the gas station. His face changes to a look I remember all too well from my own childhood. It's the look he gave me right before ...

"Are you okay?"

Thorn's voice startles me. I shake my head and force the memories from my mind before they get a grip on me.

"I ... I'm fine. Let's just go."

An icy chill runs through me as we pull out of the gas station and head toward home.

"Your grandfather's there, so let's grab your stuff from your house before he gets home."

I agree, and we head to my house. He pulls to the curb, and I run into the house, grab a few outfits, stuff them in my backpack, and we're on our way.

Chapter Five

My grandfather's face haunts my dreams. I wake several times during the night, gasping as though I've been running. But running from what? My grandfather? Even though I'm safe at Thorn's house, the thought of him being in our house makes my stomach churn.

I spend the weekend helping Thorn and his grandfather with their lawn business. It's hard work, and at the end of the day I feel exhausted, but it's good exhaustion and comes with a sense of satisfaction.

Thorn's grandfather smiles at me. "I might just have to hire you this summer."

I grin. "I wouldn't mind that at all."

After school on Monday, Coach Jones stands facing us, hands behind his back. "Congratulations on making the South Bay High girls' track team. I want the best and the fastest on my team—the ones filled with fire."

He walks from one end of the bleachers and back, looking straight ahead, brows furrowed, then turns to face us. "That being said, I don't need anyone who can't work as part of a team. I don't accept attitude on my team ... unless it's a good attitude ... a winning attitude. So, if you don't have that, now is the time to leave."

Coach Clark is standing a few feet behind Coach Jones, arms crossed, a scowl on her face, glaring at the coach's back.

Kendra, Leila, and Zoey look at each other. Leila dramatically rolls her eyes. She leans toward Zoey. "We have fire all right. Look at that fire in Coach Clark's eyes."

Coach Jones continues. "Work hard, give a hundred percent,

and do it with a good attitude. That makes you a winner to me, no matter the outcome. So, let's start our first track practice. We only have a little over a week until our first meet."

He reads the names of girls to go to high jump with Coach Clark. I'm on the list—I follow her and the other girls to the pit area.

Before we start the high jump, Coach Clark has us do a series of warm-ups with high knees. These are followed by pop-ups, arching our backs as we go backward over the bar. I easily clear the bar, and relief floods me. This is something I'm good at. Maybe it's a new start for me. A chance to prove myself.

After the pop-ups, Coach Clark raises the bar to demonstrate how she wants us to jump, approaching the bar at a curve and driving her knee upward. She makes it look easy as she arches her back and clears the bar, landing neatly in the center of the pit.

Coach Clark hadn't been paying much attention as we did our warm-up drills, but now she's focused on each jumper. She motions for me to go. I make it easily over the bar on the first few jumps and push myself as the bar inches up. As in tryouts, Sasha James and I are the last two left. I make it over 5'4" this time but go out at 5'5". Sasha makes it another two inches. Coach Clark studies me. What is she thinking?

I walk over to the long jump pit, and Sasha joins me. "Good job. Maybe we'll be jumping together this year."

I grin. "That would be fun, but this is all new to me."

"You've never done track before?"

"No, but I freerun ... like parkour."

Sasha nods. "I've seen that on YouTube."

We turn our attention to long jump. I gain six inches in long jump, missing at sixteen feet even. Sasha beats me by a foot, but Jordyn, a tall junior with long hair pulled into a ponytail, out-jumps both of us. I pass on the chance to try discus or shot put, so Coach Clark sends me over to the track with the other girls who aren't doing those events either.

At the track, Coach Jones is having girls run 3200 meters—about two miles. I sit on the grass while I wait for my turn. The sun shines on us, and I wipe sweat from my forehead as I try to shut out the thoughts crowding my mind.

It's my turn to run, and I try to run strong the whole way, saving a little extra for the end. I come in at 13:12.3. I'm not first, but I'm not last either. Still, I'll have to do better if I want to be taken as a serious runner.

Coach Jones whistles for us to come to the bleachers. I notice Jordyn sitting at the end of the second bleacher and sit next to her. She turns to me. "Good job on high jump. You really nailed it."

Heat creeps up my neck. Compliments are new. "Thanks."

Coach Jones scans the bleachers, making eye contact with each of us. He looks at the clipboard and calls out eight names. I'm one of them. "Take your places on the track and let's see what you've got for the 200-meter." I rise and walk onto the track.

I'm not a sprinter. I look at the other girls in this heat. Michaela and Sasha will be fastest. I'm not sure about the others. I don't know them.

Coach blows the whistle, and we take off in a collective burst of energy. Michaela and Sasha set a fast cadence, leading the way. They reach their top speed, knees high, running tall. I try to pace myself with them but lag seconds behind. I cross the line at 32.09 seconds, third place for this heat.

Coach rotates runners until everyone has run, some more than once, and he has the eight fastest sprinters on the track. Even after running the 200-meter several times, Michaela and Sasha are still in front. Surprisingly, Kendra is one of the fastest eight also.

Coach Jones has them sit in the bleachers. He stands in front, hands behind him as though he's thinking. "That was a good job. But good isn't going to win meets. We need to be great. We need perseverance. Push on even when you feel like quitting."

Leila raises her hand and shoots him a smile. "Is that how you won *Running Free?*"

He faces her and lifts an eyebrow. "Is this about me? I think we all know I pushed through. This is about you girls. You don't have to run through a jungle or battle bugs the size of fighter planes, but you will be going up against girls who are taller, stronger, and faster. Stay the course. Push on."

Leila gives him a flirty grin. "So how did you do that?"

Coach Jones puts a fist to his chin, other arm still crossed in front of him. "For me? It was a God thing. He gave me the gift of running. But it's up to me to use it well. I kept my focus on him. I knew people all over the United States would be watching the show each week, and I wanted to be able to give God credit for all I accomplished."

Leila rolls her eyes, but the grin is still on her face.

Coach Jones leans forward, placing a foot on the bottom bleacher. "Don't knock it until you try it, as the old saying goes."

Zoey jabs Leila in the ribs with her elbow. "Yeah, time to try some religion." She snickers.

I clench my jaw and stare at my feet. How long is Coach going to let Zoey and Leila waste time?

Coach Jones resumes his pacing. Maybe he thinks best when he's moving. "So, if we're done getting off track—pun intended— then let's get on with things. Coach Clark is going to take over for a bit and work on relays while I check on the boys."

Coach Clark walks to the front. "It's time we get back to business. Unlike Coach Jones, I have no glory stories. It takes hard work to win." Frowning, she looks directly into Leila's eyes. "Everyone find a place to sit in the grass by the track."

A sigh slips out as I take a seat. It's going to be a long afternoon.

After practice, Thorn and I drive to his house. As soon as we open the door, a delicious aroma wafts our way. As we eat, I glance around the table at Thorn and his grandparents. They haven't had an easy life, but they still seem happy. like they belong together. And for now, I belong too. My mood lightens. Even science homework doesn't seem so bad doing it with Thorn. Finally, I close the book. Enough for today. I turn to Thorn. "Let's freerun."

He looks up. "Didn't you get enough running at track practice?"

"I like freerunning better. I can do whatever I want."

Thorn grins. "Feeling a little wild tonight?"

"Distracted. And tired of running by the rules. I need a chance to be creative. When you freerun, it's pure adrenaline, but it's also like a dance."

"My freerunning looks like ballet to you?"

I laugh. I want to say yes, but I punch him on the arm instead. "Come on, let's go."

Thorn takes off at a jog. I follow. We run toward the playground the way we have for years. Thorn stops suddenly, and I end up bumping into him. "What?"

He points. The playground is now surrounded by a standard chain link fence. Judging from how Thorn's height compares to it, it's a six-foot fence. We approach it. "Where's the entrance?" I ask.

"Don't know." Thorn starts jogging around the perimeter. The only entrance is where the steps lead onto the playground. A large padlock secures the gate.

I kick at the grass and mutter a word I don't normally use. "Now I really want to freerun." A thought races through my mind. "You know, a fence has never stopped us before. That's what freerunning is all about."

"And if we're seen?" Thorn asks.

"We run fast?"

Thorn nods. "Okay."

"We going to climb it?"

Thorn shakes his head. "Gate vault."

I nod. We use that to flip over walls or fences too high to jump. Thorn runs at the fence and jumps, landing near the top of the fence. He pulls up and leans over almost like he's going to drop headfirst on the other side. He grabs the fence low on the far side, kicks his legs up, and twists over, dropping to the ground. I follow.

Thorn turns to me. "Follow the leader?"

Just like Thorn to try and distract me from what's bothering me. "Sure."

I follow Thorn as he sprints toward the wooden play set in the center of the playground and dives through the tire swing, does two forward rolls, then goes up on his hands and walks on them. I laugh. I love when he's playful. His relaxed mood calms me.

After two rounds of running the playground, vaulting and climbing our way across the equipment, Thorn loops around behind the wall that hides the dumpster and shed. He runs up the side of the shed, cat-grabs the top, and wall climbs up. I cat-grab, but my feet slide as I try to wall-climb. Thorn reaches down, grasps my wrist, and pulls me up.

We sit side by side on the shed, no need to talk. The roar of engines fills the air, and I turn toward the sound. Two trucks are racing down the road. Didn't they see the dead-end sign? They'll end up hitting the chain link fence that runs behind the convenience store. If they tear through it, they'll hit the dumpster behind the store or the store itself. I don't want to look, but I can't tear my gaze away. I reach in my pocket and wrap my hand around my Statue of Liberty souvenir coin, rubbing it between my thumb and first finger.

Sirens pierce my ears, and three police cars turn onto the road, blue lights flashing.

Thorn stands to get a better view. "Wonder what's going on?"

I stand next to him. "Don't know. It's not good, though."

A squeal of tires fills the air, followed by the sound of metal ripping through metal as the first truck tears through the fence, scraping the post as it goes. A loud crash of glass and metal fills the air as the second truck smashes into the first. A shiver runs through me. My head throbs, the crash still ringing in it. I clasp my hands to my temples. The police cars pull over, one to the left and one to the right of the trucks. The third pulls crossways behind the wreck.

Six officers emerge from the three cars and surround the trucks, guns drawn like a movie. The last officer turns and surveys the surroundings. He looks right at us. My breath catches. Can they see us in the dark? Are we illuminated by the flashing lights?

"Down." Thorn's voice is terse. "We have to get out of here."

We jump from the building to the dumpster and then the ground.

Adrenaline rushes through me. "We can't go back out onto the road."

"This way." Thorn runs at the part of the fence blocked from view of the road by the wall and does a gate vault, landing on the other side. Energy pumps through me as I follow, easily clearing the wall.

Thorn runs along the fence in the opposite direction from the road. I follow him up the hill and around to the other side of the school. He slows so we can jog side by side. "We'll go this way. It's longer, but we won't be seen by the police."

My breathing slows as we near Thorn's house. "I wonder what was going on with the trucks."

"Don't know. It should be on the news tonight though."

"No way I'm going to be able to settle down now."

Thorn turns to me. "Where do you want to go?"

"I can't think of anywhere other than the mill district. It's not that far."

"Or that safe. Especially at night."

"Please? I'm going crazy."

Thorn nods. "Okay. But I don't like the idea ... and we're driving."

We arrive in the mill district, and Thorn pulls into the parking lot of a two-story factory that has been closed for several hours. The brick factory has windows with narrow metal ledges and bars over the glass. There's a front entrance, a side entrance, and a loading dock that runs the length of the back. Two large trucks are parked in front, backed up as though they just unloaded their goods. One set of stairs leads up to the dock, and two large sliding padlocked metal doors open into what is probably a warehouse for the factory.

Glass from broken security lights crunches under our feet as we walk. Thorn slows. I hear a rustling from a dumpster ahead and freeze. A cat streaks by me, and I let out a shriek. Thorn laughs, but I sense the nervousness he's trying to mask.

I swallow. "Come on. Let's go." I run toward a low wooden rail fence around a garden that divides the parking lot from the sparse grass in front of the factory. It's probably someone's attempt to make the area look better. I grasp the fence with both hands and throw my legs over sideways. I land on the lawn and do a series of front flips across it. My muscles respond, and it feels right.

Freeing. Several yards ahead, three stairs lead to a metal door, the side entrance to the factory. I run up the steps, grasp the safety rail with my arms placed shoulder-width apart, swing my legs between my arms, and easily clear the rail landing on the ground below. There's a wall ahead. Should I do a tic tac? A wall spin? I'm not going to try a wall flip and risk landing on my rear in front of Thorn. A tic tac it is. As I run toward the wall, the image of my grandfather staring at the little kids at the church fills my mind. I need to push myself harder.

I grit my teeth and focus on the brick wall ahead of me. I sprint toward it, bend my knees, jump, and hit the wall feet first, then come back off at a higher angle, landing on the loading dock of the warehouse.

Thorn hits the wall behind me and lands next to me on the loading dock. I dash the length of the concrete dock toward a dumpster and make the leap, landing on the outer edge. The stench burns my nose as I execute a series of front walkovers, then flip off the other end.

Thorn passes me. His nervousness has been replaced by adrenaline. Using some fancy moves, he jumps forward onto a first-floor window ledge. I follow, but I slow down when I see him ready to leap onto a window ledge higher up on the building. I know freerunners do things like climb buildings and leap to other buildings, but I've never done anything like it. Thorn jumps to the window ledge and uses it to spring to another one. Thank goodness there's not another building for him to jump to.

"Thorn, come back down." My voice is shaky. It was my idea to come here, but now I'm regretting it as my stomach knots with apprehension. I reach in my pocket and rub my Statue of Liberty souvenir coin.

Thorn looks down at me. "Thought you liked being creative and not having rules."

Is he joking, or is that anger in his voice? Anger at me for some reason? I start to answer, but a black car pulls into the lot at the front of the factory and parks beside Thorn's truck. My breathing quickens. Why did I suggest coming to such a remote place? I look around for something to use as a weapon. Nothing. I pull my flip phone from my pocket and wish it were one of the fancy smart phones. Can you even call 9-1-1 on these cheap phones?

In the dim glow of a distant streetlight, I see Thorn look toward me and then toward the car.

As the car door opens, Thorn jumps back to the wall where I'm still standing. A man walks toward us. I clutch Thorn's hand but release it as I recognize the approaching figure. "Coach Jones!" I gasp. "Holy … you scared the crap out of me! What are you doing here?"

He strides toward the wall, and I drop to the lower wall and then the parking lot. Thorn is right behind me.

Coach walks up to us, face grim. "The question is, what are you doing here? In this neighborhood and after dark?"

"We're freerunning," I say. "It helps clear my mind."

"I recognize the moves. I freerun myself. What I meant is, what are you doing here?" He locks gazes with me. I look away. "I recognize you both from the track team, don't I?"

I nod.

"Do your parents know where you are?"

I shrug. "Only got a mom, and she doesn't care much where I am. She knows I'm with Thorn." I gesture toward him.

Coach turns his attention to Thorn. "What about your parents?"

Thorn crosses his arms. He's trying to look tough. This is so not like Thorn. "Live with my grandparents. They don't ask me where I'm going every time I walk out the door."

Coach is silent for a few seconds. Then he shifts his weight to his back foot and rubs his chin with one hand. "This isn't a safe neighborhood." He looks toward Thorn. "And what I saw you doing wasn't safe at all, not to mention you're trespassing."

Thorn stands up to his full height. My heart crumples a little. Thorn only acts like this when he feels challenged. He faces Coach Jones. "Then why are you here?"

Thankfully, Coach ignores the attitude and chooses to answer. "I volunteer at the open gym program at the Mill District City

Church some evenings." He gestures toward the church I'd noticed when Thorn gassed his truck. "Play basketball with the preteens mostly. Sometimes I help with a tumbling program they have for grade school kids if they're short of volunteers. Besides, I don't live too far from here."

Thorn huffs through his nose. "A reality TV star? And you live here?" He says it as a question, but it sounds like a challenge.

Coach studies Thorn. "What's wrong with that? Rent's cheap, and I lived here at one time. I'd rather put my money into something more meaningful than an expensive apartment."

"You lived here?" I asked. "In the mill district?"

"Yes, but we were talking about you."

Thorn is glowering. This isn't the Thorn I know.

Coach makes eye contact with him. "I'm not the enemy. I'm concerned about you being here at night. Is this where you always freerun?"

He's looking at Thorn, but I answer. "No. We used to run at the elementary school, but they fenced it in. There's Willow Street Park, but it's trashy, and it's known as a hangout for teens smoking weed."

Coach looks thoughtful. "You need a safer place. I'll look around and see if I can find one for you."

Thorn laughs, but it's not a friendly laugh. "You won't find one. Not around here."

Coach nods. "Maybe we can set something up at the church. The tumbling program only goes to fifth grade. On Friday nights, we have open gym for sixth to eighth grade, but that's all we have for older kids. We need something more. Maybe a freerunning club?"

A spark of hope lights Thorn's face, then it's gone. "We don't have money for something like that. Don't have much time either by the time I work my job, go to track practice, and do my homework."

"We'd find sponsors for it, so it would be free like the other programs at the church." Coach meets Thorn's gaze. "You two could help get it going. I might be able to show you a thing or two. And I could probably learn a few things from you. What do you say?"

"Really? A freerunning club? That would be great." I turn to Thorn. "Right, Thorn?"

He frowns. "If they let him. Little kids are one thing. Teens from the poor side aren't all cute like that. Besides, there's still my job."

I stare at Thorn. He's usually the hopeful one. The one who believes everything will turn out okay because of his belief in God. But this time I'm the hopeful one. Something's up.

Coach faces Thorn. "Is something bothering you? Might as well say it. You're not going to hurt my feelings."

Thorn starts to speak, then hesitates. "Nothing is wrong. It sounds good. Too good. Stuff like that doesn't happen for us."

Coach lifts an eyebrow. "But you'd be part of a freerunning club for teens if I could make it happen?"

He shrugs. "Sure. I guess."

I let out a breath.

Coach glances at his watch. "It's getting late. I'll see you both at practice tomorrow."

Thorn looks at me. "Come on, let's go."

I say goodnight to Coach and follow Thorn to his truck. "What's up? You weren't acting yourself at all with Coach. Don't you like him?"

"Well enough, but he didn't have a right to question us about being in the mill area."

"He's our coach. He's concerned about us. And having a freerunning club would be fun."

"I'm not getting my hopes up."

I stop. "You're the optimistic one, the one who always thinks things will go right for us. I'm the one who doubts. What's going on?"

"Just have a lot on my mind." Thorn is silent as he navigates the dark streets of the mill district and back to his grandparents' house. When I get out, I can still feel the tension between us, but I don't even know why. My heart sinks as he goes upstairs to bed without saying goodnight.

Chapter Six

On Wednesday, our history teacher tells us we're going to spend class time in the library working on our research papers. I started mine the weekend Thorn was visiting his dad, and I've been working on it every weekend since. It's almost done.

However, I don't have enough resources. I have online journals and websites, but not four books. The requirement is to have the actual book in hand, not read it online. I head to the history section, but it's crowded. Everyone is looking for books, so I go to the reference section and find it empty.

I'm scanning the shelves for something about the Battle of Okinawa when I spot the yearbook section. Those are reference books? They're probably there so no one will take one and then lose it. The books go back to the year the school opened. I hesitate, then pull the book from the year Mom was a freshman. I flip through it until I find the class pictures, then search the freshman class until I find her. I wonder why I haven't ever seen pictures of her from her school years?

Mom's shoulder-length brown hair is styled like most of the other girls whose pictures are on the page, and she's wearing makeup. She looks pretty and well dressed—like the popular girls. It's not what I expected. She rarely spends time on her appearance now.

I scrutinize the photo more closely. Was she from the rich side of town? Up until I was almost seven, we lived with my grandparents in the house Mom lived in when she went to high school. Was it on the rich side? I never paid attention to that kind of thing.

Images of the house start to fill my mind. I picture the yard I used to play in and my bed with a Finding Nemo comforter. My mom painted my room to look like an ocean with fish swimming in it. She redid my whole room for my sixth birthday. The day replays in my mind—me dressed in my new pink dress, excited to open my presents. I squeeze my eyes tightly shut, knowing what is coming next, and shake my head to clear the memories.

I open my eyes. I'm still holding the yearbook open. I flip to the activities page. My jaw drops. My mother was a cheerleader? Why has she never mentioned it? Apparently, everything I've pictured about her life before we moved to our current home is wrong. Suddenly the library is stuffy and too warm. I slam the book shut, locate the yearbooks for the next three years, and pull them from the shelf. I glance around and spy Thorn, sitting at a table, book open, and jotting notes on an index card. I head for the table and pull out the chair next to him. I set the four yearbooks on the table. He looks up. "What's wrong?"

"Nothing, why?"

Thorn laughs, but it sounds more like a snort. "Yeah, right. What's up?"

I hold up the first yearbook. "I found my mom in this. It was her freshman year. I think she was one of the rich kids. She was a cheerleader. No one from the poor side could afford to be a cheerleader."

He examines the photo. "She has the look. You don't know where she lived?"

I shake my head. "No. And I even lived in the same house she grew up in until first grade."

"You don't remember where it was?"

"I remember the house. And I remember it being really nice. But I never really thought about it. Rich side, poor side didn't mean anything to me. What about your parents? Wouldn't they be in these yearbooks?"

Thorn tightens his lips. He doesn't normally talk about his parents. I shouldn't have asked. Finally, he speaks. "My parents were seniors that year."

I wait.

He flips to the senior section and points to a class photo of a guy in a football jersey—Calvin Cooper. I study the photo. He has a self-confident grin as though knowing he was admired. "He was good looking."

Thorn runs his hand backward through his shortly cropped hair. "Good looking—and a football player from the rich side. My mom wasn't. She lived with my grandparents in the same house they live in now. She did okay, though. My grandparents weren't as poor as some. They were able to buy her things. She was popular and pretty. She was even on the homecoming court."

He turns the page and points to her photo. Serena Miller.

I focus on the picture. His mom was slender and blond, her eyes filled with excitement as if being on the homecoming court was the start of a bright life. I never met Thorn's mom, but I see her eyes every time I look into his. The same shape. The same shade of blue.

Thorn shuts the yearbook and pushes it toward me. I stack it with the others. "I want to, um, 'borrow' the four yearbooks from Mom's high school years so I can study them more closely," I confess.

Wordlessly, Thorn glances around and shoves the books in his drawstring bag.

Later, at the end of track practice, we meet at his truck. "I need to go by the house. I need clean clothes."

"You know Grandma will wash yours—or you can use the machine and do your own, if you prefer."

"I know. But I want something different to wear."

He pulls out of the lot and turns toward my house. I close my eyes and lean my head back. Questions fill my mind—questions that might have answers somewhere in the yearbooks.

Thorn pulls to the curb. There's no sign of my grandfather's car. If I'm lucky, he's gone for good. But Mom would have called me or Thorn's grandmother, wouldn't she?

Thorn unzips his backpack. "I'll wait here. I can start my algebra homework."

The kitchen is empty when I go in, but the sink is full of dirty dishes. I'm tempted to ignore them since I'm not living here right now, but if I leave them, who knows when they'll get washed. There'll be roaches everywhere by the time I move back in. It's Florida, after all. I run hot water and start washing.

A noise alerts me to someone in the house. I grip the plate I'm scrubbing as I turn. Mom comes into the kitchen. The dark circles under her eyes accentuate the tension etched on her face.

I rinse the plate and put it in the rack. "He's still here?"

She sighs. "He's different, Kia. He's caring and kind. He helps out, and he asks about you. All the things I wish he'd been and done before. He really wants to be your grandfather."

I attack the spaghetti pot, scrubbing furiously. "He's no grandfather to me."

She looks at me, her face filled with hurt. "Why can't you give him another chance? He wants to make a difference in his final months. I know you can't forgive him—and maybe you shouldn't. But can't you give him a chance?"

I turn from the sink. "How can you be so sure he's different? What if he's not? What if he's just fooling everyone—you included?"

Mom gives a long sigh. She picks at dried spaghetti on the table. "He's doing his best. Just let the past go. Besides ..."

I turn my back to her and walk to the sink. I lift another plate out of the hot water, scrub and rinse. I bite back angry words and take a breath before I turn to her. "Besides?"

"He said he'd help me with the bills."

My head throbs. I rub the back of my neck. "I thought we were doing okay."

"I'm always a bit behind."

She's lying. I can tell by her eyes. "What?"

She goes to the refrigerator and pulls a beer from the vegetable drawer. She opens it and takes a sip.

"Tell me." I say it louder than I meant, and she jumps.

She flicks at the can tab with her thumbnail. "Lost my job."

"Really? REALLY?"

"It wasn't my fault. The boss didn't like me. I made a mistake on a chart, and he was all over me."

"And?"

"I might have said something to him."

I sigh. Same old story. Fired—and not her fault.

"I didn't make much anyway. I already got another job at the gas station on Willow and Fifth."

"You went from working at the public health office to working at a gas station?"

"Don't matter. I never make enough no matter where I work. I want more for you than the basics. I've never been able to give you the things I grew up with. I had everything my friends had, but you don't. You could have nice clothes. A smartphone. I can't give that to you, but your grandfather can give you anything you want if you're nice to him."

"Nice to him." Her words trigger old memories. The room closes in on me. I need to get out of here. Dropping the pan into the sink, I stride toward the back door. I'll do what Thorn suggested and wash my clothes at his house. I turn back to face my mother. "You be nice to your father! I've got no reason to be. And besides, I thought he was too broke for a hotel. Now he has money to buy me a smartphone? I don't think so. I don't know what his game is, but text me when he leaves."

Yanking the back door open, I step outside and slam the door behind me.

I stop in the yard and take several breaths. The visions come—the girl in the pink dress spinning and spinning. The man saying, "You should be nice to Grandpa." The hands pulling me too close. I start to shake. I gag, and my mouth fills with acid. I lean over and put my hands on my knees.

A hand takes my arm. Thorn's voice cuts through my haze. "Come on. Let's head home. Grandma will have supper ready."

Acid still burns in my throat as I climb into Thorn's truck. I blink back tears and put a fist over my mouth to hold back a sob.

Thorn starts the truck, and we head toward his house. "You okay?"

I nod. "Yeah. It's just ... well, she says he's kind and caring and everything she used to wish he'd be."

"You think that's true?"

I shrug. "Not really. He's playing her. But it makes no difference now. He did what he did. Like I had no rights. He can't undo what he did."

Thorn nods. He gets it. We're the same that way. Only he's

determined not to let the past ruin his future, while I can't seem to move beyond the way my childhood was stolen from me. Thorn and me? We might be fifteen on the outside, but we're old on the inside.

My mood shifts as we walk into Thorn's house. The savory scent of beef stew and the unmistakable aroma of freshly baked bread wafts toward us, filling me with warmth as my stomach rumbles.

We quickly set our backpacks on the floor by the door and wash our hands at the kitchen sink. Thorn's grandma sets bowls of stew and hot crusty bread in front of me and Thorn joins us. She volunteers at the local nursing home one day a week, and she shares stories about the residents that make me feel like I really know them. I eat quickly, enjoying being part of a family, even if it's not my own.

After we're done eating, Thorn and I clear the table, then wash and dry the dishes. We clean the kitchen together, and it feels normal. Like what being part of a family should feel like. When we're done, Thorn and I sit down at the table with the yearbooks. Thorn's grandparents are watching a game show on television, the contestants shouting out answers even as I search for answers of my own.

I open the yearbook from when Mom was a sophomore. Thorn is sitting close, looking over my arm. Mom is still a cheerleader. A picture on the next page grabs my attention. Cassandra Clark! I quickly scan the captions before examining the pictures. Coach Clark was a sophomore the same year as Mom. She dominates the sports page. According to the captions, she went all the way to state for track and placed third in high jump and fourth in hurdles. I must have missed her in the freshman yearbook. I scrutinize the pictures. Standing among the winners, she proudly wears her medals on ribbons around her neck. Cassandra Clark looks young, happy, and full of hope. This is not the same Coach Clark I know. What changed her from a hopeful track star to an angry coach?

I look more closely at the photos of the track members who

went to state. Thorn leans closer. "Isn't that Coach Jones?"

I nod and read the captions aloud: "Terrence Jones, anchor 4 by 400 team, first place, 300-meter hurdles, third place."

Thorn's brows draw together. "So, he really did attend South Bay."

"You thought he was lying?"

"No, but ..."

I look up from the yearbook. "What?"

"When he was on *Running Free*, he said he and his brother grew up in Miami."

"He could have grown up there, moved here, and then moved back to Miami after high school or college."

"I guess. Is his brother in the yearbook?"

I start with the freshman class and search for him. I go on to search the sophomore, junior, and senior classes. "No one with the same last name who looks anything like him. "He's not in here, but he could have already graduated high school or still been in middle school."

I flip back to Coach Jones' track pictures. His eyes are large and full of life. His smile is confident. It's the same crooked grin, one side raised, we see every day at practice. I turn to Thorn. "What surprises me is he and Coach Clark obviously know each other. They were both in track. But she seems to dislike him. She'll say stuff like, 'Well, according to our celebrity coach,' and her tone is ... I'm not sure ... maybe condescending?"

"Huh. Wonder what's up with that." He glances at the yearbook again. "So, my parents, your mom, and two of the track coaches all went to school together."

"Great. Now I have more questions I don't have answers to."

"Like?"

"Like, was my mom from the rich side? What happened to change her so much? Why does Cassandra Clark dislike Terrence Jones so much?"

Thorn shakes his head. "I couldn't even guess, but I bet the answers would be really interesting."

Chapter Seven

I've been looking forward to track practice Thursday afternoon, especially finding out what my events will be. But from the start of practice, there's tension in the air. An assistant coach is working with the boys on field events. Coach Clark and Coach Jones are off to the side talking. Coach Jones's normal smile is missing, while anger oozes from Coach Clark.

Coach Jones turns from her and calls us together. His smile is in place, but it doesn't reach his eyes. He shakes his head as though shaking off his bad mood, scans the bleachers, and grins. This time it's for real. "Time to get down to business. We're going to be working on different events to find out what events each of you will take part in."

He looks around and points to my side of the bleachers. "Let's have everyone on this half of the bleachers go with Coach Clark for hurdles. The rest stay here with me to run. Later, I'll work with the girls who want to do discus and shot put."

I stand and head toward Coach Clark. She scowls. "Follow me. We're wasting time."

She leads us to the track where hurdles are set up. I sit on the ground. Kendra is sitting near me. She's almost bouncing with excitement. "I can't wait to jump hurdles. It looks so fun."

Leila and Zoey roll their eyes.

Coach Clark walks to the front of the group and faces us, hands on hips. "I don't want to hear anyone say they jump hurdles. You run hurdles." She walks up inches from Kendra. "It's a sprint. You don't just jump up and down over hurdles. Sasha, why don't you come up here and demonstrate?"

We watched as Sasha gracefully drives her knee up over the hurdle and easily clears it. Is there anything she can't do? At least she isn't stuck up about it. She's friendly to everyone.

Leila Ellis is up first. She takes her mark and sprints on the whistle. She tries to clear the hurdle but clips her toe on it.

"Ellis! Drive your knee up. If you drive with your toes, you're going to hit the hurdle. Get to the back of the line. Next!"

One by one the girls try the hurdles while Coach barks out instructions. Finally, I'm next. Only about a quarter of the girls have been successful, but hurdles should be easy for me with all the freerunning I do.

"Move it, Scott," Coach shouts. I glance at her. She's watching me, her mouth a hard line.

I start out fast. I'm ready when it's time to drive my knee up and extend my leg over, but I catch a glimpse of a white-haired man walking away. Heat roils in me. I know I'm not imagining it this time. Is my grandfather stalking me? I'm not paying attention, and I catch my back foot on the hurdle. I'm falling, but there's nothing I can do. I land hard on the ground and roll to my back, gravel biting into me. I roll over and get to my feet, wincing as pain goes through my ankle.

An annoying buzz of snickering and whispers reach me.

"Nice one, Scott," Leila says. She and Zoey look at each other and laugh. Kendra looks down. At least she's not laughing.

Heat rises in my neck, and my ears burn. I glare at Leila, trying to bite back a retort, but the words force themselves between my lips. "Seems to me you were the first one to mess up!" Then I call her a name I don't usually use.

I try to walk out the pain in my ankle, forcing myself to focus only on track. I might be good at this once I learn the techniques.

Coach Clark motions for me to sit next to the other girls, and Leila places her foot next to my leg, spikes pushing into my skin. "Maybe you need track cleats."

"No, she needs some skill. Cleats don't help you if you can't jump," Zoey says. She elbows Leila, and they both laugh.

Coach Clark is still watching me, so I turn sideways, my back to the triplets, and watch the others on the hurdles.

After the last attempt, Coach faces us. "Sasha, Michaela, and Katelyn are the only ones who looked like they knew what they were doing. I don't know how much simpler I can make it for the rest of you. We only have one week until the first meet. Normally, we start practices earlier in February or even January, but we got a late start with Coach Cleary having a heart attack. Then we had to wait for our celebrity coach to arrive instead of just going on with things." Her voice drips with sarcasm.

She crosses her arms and studies us. "I will demonstrate step-by-step what hurdles should look like, and you watch me. Then you're going to get in line and do it like I do."

Coach comes up to full height quickly, sprinting toward the hurdle. She drives her knee and lead leg cleanly over the hurdle, but as she brings her trail foot over sideways, she hits her ankle on the hurdle. The hurdle falls, and Coach Clark tumbles to the ground with it, landing hard. My jaw drops. Did that really happen?

Leila gives a burst of laughter. "You sure you want us to do it like that? Cause that looks pretty much like what Kiana did."

Kendra looks at Leila, eyes wide, but Zoey grins.

Coach Clark rolls over and pushes to a squat, pauses, then slowly stands and brushes her hands down her legs. She strides to stand in front of Leila, her nostrils flaring. She plants her feet wide, hands on hips, and looks down at the trio sitting by the track. Her eyes fix on Leila. "Get yourself off my track, and don't come back." She points to the gate leading from the track area to the parking lot.

Leila stands and straightens her running shorts. She faces Coach Clark. "My dad's on the school board. He said you got passed over for head coach." She smirks. "Guess it smarts to have them hire an outside coach instead of giving it to you." She looks down at Zoey and Kendra. "Come on, let's get out of here."

Zoey hops up, but Kendra hesitates before she stands. She looks first at Leila and Zoey, then at Coach Clark.

Coach Clark addresses her. "You go with them, you don't come back. Would be a shame. You're a good runner."

Kendra slowly sits back down and drops her gaze.

Leila sneers. "You stay here, you're done with us. You choose. Her or us?"

I'm glad it's not me she's talking to. I've never understood all the rules of girl politics.

Kendra remains sitting, eyes down, as Leila and Zoey turn and walk away without looking back. A tear trickles down Kendra's face. I start to say something but have no idea what to say, so I turn my attention back to Coach Clark, glad I'm not Kendra. I don't think her buddies are going to let this drop.

Coach sets the hurdle back up, and we line up again. I focus and visualize myself going over it. It's no harder than the vaults I do, and I've gone over higher obstacles. This time I easily clear it. I glance toward Coach Clark. Did she notice?

Coach is watching me, expression blank. "You've never done track at all?"

I shake my head. "No."

She studies me. "Are you related to Melonie Scott?"

"She's my mom."

Coach Clark studies me, a slight sneer on her face. My breathing quickens. I don't know what to say, so I turn to join the others waiting for their turns.

My mind spins into gear. So Coach Clark did know my mom. By the look on her face, I'd guess they weren't friends. Did she know Mom got pregnant right after graduation? Is she looking down on Mom for being a teen mother?

Coach Jones returns with the other team members and calls us all to the bleachers. "We're done for today. Good job, everyone. Get as much sleep as possible tonight because you're going to need your energy tomorrow." He holds up a pile of papers. "I have the track meet schedule. Get one on your way out and stick it on your refrigerator once you get home, so your parents see it."

Thorn and I do homework together, which makes it go a lot faster. I shut my history book and look at the clock—9:00 p.m. "Could we go to my house to get the stuff I didn't get last time?"

He nods. "But if your grandfather is there, I'm going in with you."

"If he's there, I'm going in through my window, and he'll never know I was there."

Thorn shakes his head. "Sad to have to sneak into your own

house."

Thank goodness my grandfather's car isn't there when we pull up. "Wonder where he is? Seems like if he has cancer, he'd be home resting."

"Just be glad he's not here. I'll be right here."

I grab my track schedule and take it in. I clip my schedule to the fridge with a magnet. Mom is sitting at the table alone, two empty Miller Lite cans beside her.

I walk over to the table. "You okay?"

She looks up at me, flicking the can tab with a nail. "Yeah. Just thinking."

I pull out a chair and sit. "About what?"

She shrugs. "Oh, nothing important. Just ... well, sometimes life doesn't turn out like you hope. When you're young, you have all these great plans."

My brain clicks into gear. "Plans like what?"

She flips the tab a few more times. Is she going to answer? She sighs. "Life was different when I was young. I thought I was in love with someone."

"What made you think about it now?"

"I guess it just hit me that you're in high school now. I see you and Thorn together. Not so long ago, I thought I was in love with someone."

I ignore the part about Thorn, deciding not to correct her assumption. "Was that someone my dad?"

"Doesn't matter. It was a long time ago. I was a different person. Besides, my father would never have heard of it, him being black and all."

"Why would that matter? No one cares about that kind of thing."

"My father did. He had a lot to say about it."

"Figures," I mutter. I search for something to say, and it hits me. This is my chance to bring up the yearbooks. "One day when I was in the library, I saw the old yearbooks. Flipped through some of them."

"The ones from when I was in high school?"

I nod. "I was surprised to see you were a cheerleader."

Mom flicks the can tab a few more times before answering. "That was your grandmother's doing. Your grandfather thought I should do something more beneficial with my time."

"But your mom let you be a cheerleader?"

"Yes. She convinced him it would look good for him to have a daughter who was a cheerleader. Image was everything to him. He liked the prestige of owning his own business, and she played on that to get him to agree."

I nod. "Of course, you lived on the rich side if he owned a business. I never thought about that. I guess I pictured you growing up in this neighborhood."

There's a movement at the back door. My grandfather steps into the kitchen, eyes boring into me. My heartbeat quickens. How long has he been here? Why didn't I hear his car pull in or the door open? A lofty look fills my grandfather's face. "Me live in this neighborhood? Hardly."

"You live here now," I point out.

"To be near you and your mother. And because that pathetic room they called an apartment at Oaklawn Assisted Living Facility was a disgrace. There's no way I could have lived there."

My mouth drops open. "They offered you an apartment, and you turned it down?"

Before he can answer, the door opens, and Thorn steps into the kitchen. The look on his face says he's ready to defend me if need be.

My grandfather glances at him, then turns away as though dismissing his presence. "I'm going to live here with you. Your mom's job doesn't pay enough. She needs my help, and I need a place to live. It works out well for both of us. Family takes care of family." He looks at me, his eyes daring me to say something.

"I thought you were sick. Had cancer. Needed care. What happened to that?"

He speaks in a slow, controlled tone. "I'll hire a nurse when the time comes. Until then, is it unreasonable to want to be with family? To expect a little loyalty?"

"Loyalty? Loyalty for what?"

"For letting your mother and you stay in my house. You lived under my roof and ate my food. Now it's your turn." His eyes bore into mine, and I look away. He leans toward me, his nostrils flaring, and Thorn steps forward, placing himself between my grandfather and me. For a long moment, I think my grandfather is going to do something. Maybe even hit Thorn. Instead, he glares at me.

"Loyalty is clearly not a word you understand. In any case, this is a family matter. We'll discuss it again when there are no outsiders sticking their nose in." He glares at Thorn. "Meantime, I'm going to bed. It's been a long day."

He leaves the room. The instant he's out of sight, Mom grabs another can of beer from the fridge and pops the top. "I know you're not happy with your grandfather here. I know he hurt you in the past. But he's changed. He'd never hurt you now."

"Maybe not in the same way. But to have to be in the same house as him ..."

Mom sighs. "Give him a chance, okay? Living here with us is new to him too. But he's willing to make it work. Can you at least try for me? One wrong move, and I'll boot him out. Promise."

My mind races. I glance over at Thorn. He's watching me. I can't live with Thorn forever. Or can I? My mouth goes dry, and I walk to the refrigerator and pull out the orange juice carton. It's almost empty. I drink the last few sips, crush the container, and throw it in the trash. Then, I turn and walk out the back door, followed by Thorn. Halfway to the truck, I realize that my grandfather's appearance interrupted the conversation with Mom about her high school years, and I hadn't yet asked her about the others who attended South Bay at the same time she did. And I didn't get my stuff.

The emotions of the day have drained me, so I quickly change to pajamas, grab a blanket, and settle on the couch. Thorn has offered to sleep on the couch and let me have his room, but I refused. It wouldn't be right. Besides, I like the couch. I start to drift off to sleep but wake back up, my mind working hard to process everything I've learned.

Finally, I fall asleep—and then the dreams start. The little girl in the pink dress, spinning and spinning. Him watching and leering. Then it switches, and I'm at track practice spinning in the pink dress while Coach Clark watches and laughs an eerie laugh. I run and run, but everywhere I go, she's there laughing. She reaches out for me, but as she grabs me, she turns into my grandfather, who laughs louder as I try to get away. I scream and wake up tangled in my quilt.

I drift in and out of sleep. Just as dawn is breaking, I hear a phone ringing.

Chapter Eight

Lights go on upstairs, and footsteps move rapidly over my head. Muffled voices reach me. The words grow louder. Thorn is arguing with his grandmother. I sit up and strain to hear what it is about, but the voices grow quiet.

Footsteps come down the stairs, and Thorn appears in the living room, dressed and wearing his backpack. His jaw is clenched, and anger lines his face.

"What is it?" I ask, knowing it's going to be bad.

"My dad," he says through clenched teeth. "He got beat up bad."

"At 5:45 in the morning?"

Thorn shrugs. "Don't know. Don't know why they couldn't wait a couple more hours to call. Grandma wants to go right now."

"You're leaving? Can I go too?"

Thorn looks away, and now I know what they were fighting about. I'm not going. I have to go home. I blink back tears. It couldn't last forever, but I was hoping it would last until I thought of another way to avoid my grandfather.

Thorn's grandmother descends the stairs, small suitcase in hand. "I'm sorry about this. I've already called your mom to let her know we'll be dropping you off. If there was any other way ..."

Not trusting my voice, I nod, blinking back tears. Of course, it was too good to last.

A few minutes later, we climb into Thorn's grandparents' car and head for my house. A light is on in the kitchen.

"You want me to walk up with you?" Thorn's grandfather asks.

I shake my head and climb out of the car, then lean back in. "Thanks for letting me stay."

"Sure thing," Thorn's grandfather says. "We'll be praying for you. And your grandfather too. For a changed heart."

I want to say something. Anything. To let him know he's wasting his prayers as far as my grandfather is concerned. But I stay silent, not wanting to hurt his feelings.

Thorn promises to text later. I turn and walk slowly to the house, open the back door, and slip in. Mom is at the table, still in her pajamas, hands wrapped around a mug of coffee. It's barely 6:00 a.m. I walk into the living room, drop onto the couch, and click the television remote. An early morning news show is on. Mom joins me, and we sit in silence until it's time to get ready for the day.

The day creeps by minute by minute. I keep checking for a text from Thorn, but nothing. Finally, the dismissal bell rings. There's no meet this Saturday, and there's no track practice this Friday, because Coach says we'll have to work extra hard next week, so we get a day off now.

I don't want to go home yet, so I keep jogging until I find myself headed to the mill district. The noxious chemical smell assaults my nose long before I enter the area.

Mill District City Church is ahead, and the lights are on. I slow my jog as I near it. I bite my bottom lip. I want to go in, but I'm not sure if I should just walk in without being invited. Coach wouldn't mind. After all, he did invite me. But is Coach there now? Would he give up Friday nights to work with kids?

I slow to a walk as the church comes into sight. It can't hurt to take a look. I freeze when I spot a man with all-too-familiar white-hair walking out of the church entrance. First my school and now this church? No, it can't be. I'm losing it, imagining my grandfather every time I see someone with white hair.

I jog the last block to the church for a better look. No, I'm not imagining things. It really is my grandfather. My heart begins to thud painfully against my chest when I see he has a child by the hand. It's the same little girl with dark, curly hair and light-brown skin he was watching from the gas station.

I look around. I need to tell someone. There's an older, gray-haired woman standing just inside the church doors. Doesn't she see him with the little girl?

I hesitate. I need to warn her about my grandfather, but what do I say? That my grandfather may hurt the girl? Would she believe me? Probably not, but I have to do something.

I hurry to the door and go inside. I walk up to the older woman. Her name tag reads "Carolyn Simmons, Director." I speak to her. "The man there. With that girl. Do you know him?"

She follows my gaze. "Oh, Walter Scott. Of course, I know him."

"You do? How do you know him?"

She fixes me with a look that says she thinks it's none of my business. "From here, of course."

"Here?" I echo. "He works here?"

"Volunteers. And we certainly need more like him. So many of our kids don't have grandparents, and they've taken to him. Like Isabella, the little sweetie he's walking to the car. Her mom is a single parent and sometimes has to work late."

My mind spins. He's a volunteer? Already? I look back toward him. He opens a car door, helps the little girl into the car, and closes the door after her. Then he smiles and waves as the car pulls from the curb. He turns and walks toward the playground area. It seems innocent enough, but I'm not ready to believe it is.

I'm not sure what to do. Do I stay and ask him what's going on or leave? I decide to leave. After all, I don't have any experience with church. I haven't been in church more than the few times I've gone with Thorn and his grandparents. Why did I come here anyway? I'll wait until Thorn can come. He knows more about churches. I pull the door open and head back down the sidewalk.

"Kiana."

I turn and see Coach Jones in the doorway. "I thought I saw you walking up. Are you here to check out the program?"

I shrug. "I was going to, but ..."

"But what?"

"I wasn't sure if I should. I don't have much experience with church or God."

"That's okay. You're welcome. Come on in and meet the kids I work with. The sixth, seventh, and eighth graders will be arriving any time now. Our current program only goes through eighth grade."

I follow Coach into the church gym, which looks pretty much like a school gym, with bleachers on one side and a small stage on the other. There's a hallway next to the stage. Besides the large entrance with two sets of glass doors that I just came in, there is a single set of glass doors that lead into a big room with tables and a metal door that must lead outside.

I turn my attention back to the gym. Thick blue mats cover most of the floor. Wedges, cones, and squares for tumbling are scattered on one half, and a group of boys are shooting baskets at one end of the gym.

Coach blows a whistle, and the action stops. All eyes turn to Coach. "Take a seat," he says. The boys move to the bleachers. Coach walks over to them, and I follow, unsure of what to do.

A mixture of races are represented, different shades of brown with a few white kids too. Coach stands in front of them and crosses his arms. "This is Kiana. She's a freerunner."

A boy in baggy basketball shorts, tank top, and high tops asks Coach a question in Spanish. I recognize "Que?" but that's it.

Coach looks him in the eyes. "Don't judge her until you see her moves. And speak English so she can understand you. And Chance? You might want to tie those shorts a little tighter before you lose them."

I grin. Coach understands these kids. He addresses them. "I want to start a freerunning club for you. I think it'll be fun, and there's lot we can do with it." He turns to me. "Maybe you can show these guys a move or two."

Chance springs to his feet and faces Coach. "I already got moves. You think that girl has more moves than me?" He turns to me. "You got some moves, chica?" He gives me a smug smile.

Coach meets his gaze. "Let's show some respect here, Chance. Sit down and watch. You might be impressed."

"Doubt it," he mutters under his breath.

Coach turns to me. "Can you do a few moves on the mats, or

do you need something else?"

I glance around. What can I do to impress these guys? "Can you set one of the bigger squares on end? And put one of the thick mats against the wall?"

Coach looks across the bleachers. "Travis, Drake, Rob, you guys help me."

Three of the tallest boys join Coach on the gym floor. One is white, two are light brown. They look bored, but they do as Coach tells them.

I study the layout while they make the changes I ask for. It's simple, but it'll work.

"Ready?" Coach asks.

I nod and glance toward the bleachers at a group of boys trying to look bored. Their eyes betray them. They are interested but waiting to be impressed. The girls are sizing me up. I know the look.

I head toward the largest foam cylinder picking up speed as I near it. I stop, but use the momentum to lift my body into the air, flipping over the cylinder without using my hands. I land and do three forward flips before changing direction, aiming for a large square. I jump at it, legs outstretched. My hands are behind me, and I push off the square with them as I go over it, leading with my legs for a dash vault. I grin. Nailed it.

I run toward the mat against the wall. If Thorn was here, he'd do a back flip off it, but I don't chance it. I jump at the wall, plant my hands, spin over them and land in a crouch on the ground. I roll over my shoulder and up onto my feet. I run toward Coach and do a series of front flips, landing beside him.

Chance jumps to his feet and crosses his arms, trying to look cool. "Aw, man! I thought she was going to show us some moves, not some kindergarten tumbling."

I grin. His expression gives him away. He's impressed.

Coach chooses to ignore him and instead looks at the group. "Freerunning is all about moving, never stopping. It's about training your body and controlling your movements. You want to do what Kiana did? You listen to me, follow the safety rules, and be willing to learn."

One of the boys who helped with the mats motions for Coach's attention. He's light brown, and his hair and lips tell me he's part African American.

"Yes, Drake?"

"We still gon' shoot baskets?"

Coach nods. "We'll shoot baskets, but give freerunning a try, okay? I think you'll like it. Let's try an easy skill tonight to give you an idea of what you can do."

Coach grabs the large square I used for the dash vault and moves it to the middle of the mat. "Let's start with a basic side vault. Kiana, you want to demonstrate?"

I stand at the edge of the mat, facing the square. Coach narrates as I sprint toward the block and easily clear it. I show them again, running at the block, planting my hands, jumping up and swinging my legs sideways over the block. "This is a basic vault, and you can do it over almost anything—a low wall, a bench, a handrail."

Chance springs to his feet and looks toward me. "Can you do that over like ... a car?"

I shake my head. "I can't, but my friend Thorn can. And Coach Jones probably can too."

Coach nods. "A small car, but a car, yeah. It's doable. But for now, let's work with these foam blocks."

It's not much of a challenge for the bigger guys. They probably use this move to jump over things without even thinking about it. One of the girls catches on quickly too. After everyone has had a few tries, Coach Jones calls the group together.

"Let's get quiet now." Coach clasps his hands behind him as the gym grows silent. "Earlier, you saw Kiana flip over the cylinder tumbler and vault over the block. These things might have been obstacles to the rest of us, but she knew how to overcome them." Coach pauses and makes eye contact with several of the guys in front of him.

"We all face obstacles every day. It might be a math problem you can't solve. It might be a problem with a teacher or parent. The obstacle might be something that's happening in your home. Here's the good news." Coach holds up a finger and waits to make sure everyone is listening. "God will help you overcome whatever obstacle you are facing. He promises to find a way to take the junk and use it for his own good. When you think you can't overcome what's holding you back, ask God to help you, to show you the way."

I watch Coach's face as he talks. He really believes what he's saying. I don't know. God helps us overcome obstacles? I wish that were true, but it doesn't feel that way to me.

Coach dismisses the kids, and they run back onto the court. Several of them divide into teams, and the others watch as the competition starts.

I sniff. Good smells are coming from the kitchen. I sniff again. It's some kind of meat with a savory smell. Meatloaf maybe?

Coach laughs. "They have a free meal for the homeless on Friday and Saturday nights, along with a chapel service."

I should count as homeless now that I'm not staying at Thorn's. No one is home most of the time to cook for me.

Coach grabs a mat and drags it to the wall. I help him lift it and fasten the straps over big hooks. He turns to me. "That wasn't so bad, right?"

"It was kind of fun, but I'm glad I'm not in charge."

"They can be a handful. Some of them have been through so much already that they're hard to reach. But I understand where they're coming from."

I nod. There's nothing to say. I'm still working on the obstacles in my own life. I don't have the answer for anyone else. Not yet at least.

After the last child has left, Coach turns toward me. "Give you a ride?"

"I'm okay."

Coach fixes his gaze on me. "I can't let you walk home in the dark. It's no problem taking you."

"Are you allowed to drive me home?"

"We can't drive the younger children home, but with the teens they leave it up to our discretion."

I follow Coach to his car, a black Ford Edge. Coach pulls out of the church parking lot. I tell him how to get to my house, but he navigates the streets like he knows them. Maybe he does. He glances toward me. "Tell me about yourself."

"Like, what do you want to know?"

"I already know you're a freshman, you freerun, and run track. Who are you in here?" He touches his heart.

I laugh, not because it's funny, but because I don't know the answer to that question. "I'm what you said—a freerunner and a member of the track team."

Coach gives me a half grin. "That told me absolutely nothing about you."

I shrug. "There's not much to tell."

"Not true. Everyone has a story because God made each of us with a special purpose in mind."

I can't help laughing. "You sound like Thorn."

"Your freerunning friend? The one on my track team?"

I nod.

He grips the steering wheel as he turns onto Willow. His arm muscles ripple. "So, you live with your mother?"

I release a stream of air. "Now my grandfather is staying with us."

"I had some good times with my grandfather. Sometimes he was easier to talk to than my father, but I'm sensing that's not the case with your grandfather."

I sigh. "Yeah, it's not like that for me."

Coach waits, but no more words will come. He pulls up to my house. "We can talk more another time, okay? I want to hear more about who you really are."

I nod and open the car door, ready to climb out.

"And Kiana?"

I look back. "Sir?"

"Sir?"

"That's what we say here for excuse me or what."

He grins and shakes his head. "What I was going to say was, listen to your friend Thorn."

Chapter Nine

When I get home, the house is empty. I check my phone for a text from Thorn. Nothing. I send him a quick text, asking how his father is, and wait. No answer. Finally, I go to bed, but fall into fitful sleep, interrupted by dreams of my grandfather with the little girl.

I wake to the house phone ringing. I quickly grab it. It's Thorn. "Sorry. My phone is dead, but the hospital is letting me use theirs. Better so I don't use up my minutes anyway."

I smile even though he can't see me. "How's your dad? What happened?"

Thorn sighs. "He's bad. And my grandma won't leave his side. Doesn't matter he killed her daughter. She says she forgave him, and he needs us now."

We talk a few more minutes, then Thorn has to hang up. The click of the receiver triggers an emptiness in me.

I spend the day trying to work on homework, but my mind wanders, so I finally go for a jog around the neighborhood. It's dusk when I get home, and I go inside, thankful no one else is there. I've just started searching for something to eat when a familiar rumble sounds outside my house. Thorn? But he's with his family. I run to the door and look out. Thorn climbs out of his truck, pulls out a backpack, and jogs to the door. I let him in.

He grins. "Didn't your mom tell you?"

"What?"

"I'm staying with you for a few days. My turn to sleep on the couch."

My spirits soar. "Really? That's great. Mom's at work, but she still could have called and told me."

"I told Grandma I couldn't afford to miss school and track practice. Plus, I'm going to do some of Grandpa's lawn work, so he doesn't lose customers. He drove me home and then went right back."

"How are you going to manage school, track, and work?"

He shrugs. "Don't know. But it's better than sitting in a hospital room. My dad is still unconscious and doesn't know whether I'm there or not."

Thorn's face clouds over. His eyes are troubled.

"Let's freerun," I suggest.

We head outside, and I remember the playground is fenced in now. "Willow?"

Thorn agrees, and we run down the street to Willow Park. I don't want to go there, but Thorn needs this. We race by teens sitting on the ground or leaning against the swing posts, cigarettes dangling from their lips. Thorn races to the dugout and spins off the wall. He's going to hurt himself if he doesn't slow down. But I know how he feels. The wall is a safe way to release the feelings that can't be said in words. He hits the wall again, faster and harder, and then a third time.

Thorn heads toward me, building momentum. He stops and punches the ground with his feet, sending his body high into the air. He reaches his peak height and goes into a rotation for a perfect side flip. He does a series of them, and it's like watching fluid motion.

"Give it a try," he encourages.

I shake my head. "I'd probably break a leg and be out of track."

"You can use me as a prop." Thorn bends over. "Come on, roll over my back."

A laugh escapes my lips. Use Thorn as a prop to do a side flip? I guess we've done stranger things. I back up and run toward him. I launch myself to roll over his back, but I'm too low. It's more like a tackle, and we both hit the ground.

Thorn stands and brushes the dirt from his pants. "That's not quite it."

I laugh. "I was doing my Coach Clark hurdle imitation." I tell him about the track practice where Leila and Zoey ended up getting kicked off the team.

He grins. "That would have been something to see."

"I might have felt sorry for her if she hadn't yelled at me for clipping my foot on the hurdle."

We head to my house, climb the porch post to the roof, and sit by my window, backs to the wall. We're so close our arms touch, but it's a comfortable kind of touch between friends. His warm breath reaches me as he exhales.

Thorn pulls his knees to his chest and wraps his arms around them.

I glance sideways at him. He's looking off into the distance. I clear my throat. "So, what happened with your dad? The fight?"

A sigh escapes his lips. "I'm used to my dad fighting. But this time, they say he was defending a weaker prisoner, someone who would have been killed if he hadn't stepped in."

"How bad is your dad hurt?"

"Critical. Whatever that means."

I don't know what to say. Thorn is usually the one fixing everyone else's problems. The first to step up if someone needs help. If anyone could create world peace, it would be him because he thinks if people would treat each other with kindness, all wrongs would be righted.

"Do you wish now you'd written to him? Answered his letters?"

"And said what? It was okay he beat on Mom and me and killed Mom? That he got sent to prison and left me with my grandparents?" Thorn's voice gets quieter, but more forceful.

I stay silent, almost holding my breath so he'll keep talking.

He pulls his knees more tightly to his chest and props his chin on them. "I trust God has a plan that includes salvaging the cruddy parts of life, but I wonder what life would have been like if he'd been a regular dad. The kind who would teach me to catch a ball or ride a bike instead of leaving bruises on my body and lying to people about how I got them. If he's changed now, what good is it to me?"

Down the street, a child's cry rings out, followed by a loud "shut up." Then it's quiet. Just another night on Willow Street

I lean back and close my eyes. "Your grandparents are good to you."

Thorn studies his shoes. "Yeah. They are. I'm okay with it, I guess. Nothing I can do about it anyway."

His voice says otherwise. I wait for him to say more, but he's done talking about his parents. I tell him about what happened at the church.

Thorn tightens his lips, then speaks. "So, your grandfather was just walking Isabella to her mom's car?"

"It appeared that way. And Mom is convinced he's changed. But I can't shake the feeling it's not what it seems. If my grandfather is going to be at the church, it wrecks that for me. Everything is wrecked for me with my grandfather here."

Thorn faces me. "No, it's not. Don't let your grandfather win. Fight back."

I give a sad laugh. "I'm a runner, not a fighter. All I've ever been good at is running. Running from the visions, from the things that haunt me. Running from the things I can't beat or change."

Thorn leans back against the house and looks up into the sky. "I don't have the answers, but God does. You and me? We can let things in our past hold us back, or we can embrace who we're meant to be. It's hard. You think I don't know that? But you have to stop running from what you can't change and run toward who you're meant to be."

"And if I don't know who that is?"

"I don't have that answer either. Not for you. Not for me. That's one of those things we have to trust God to answer. But right now? You need to talk to your mom. Or someone who can help."

"About my grandfather and me or about that little girl?"

"Both."

"And say what?"

"The truth."

"It sounds easy when you say it, but who is going to believe me over him?" Even as I ask it, I know the answer. No one. No one is going to believe a fifteen-year-old girl over a Santa Claus-clone retired businessman who is volunteering his time with little kids. Maybe Mom is right, and he's changed. But how safe are those little girls at the church if he hasn't?

Chapter Ten

Monday morning, I enter the school. Thorn is right behind me. Kendra is standing in front of her locker with a group of kids gathered around her. Several girls are holding their noses and making exaggerated gagging noises. The stench reaches me before I get near her locker. I put my hand over my mouth and nose. My eyes start to water as the rancid smell intensifies. Only two people I know could have been this cruel.

I meet her gaze, and she heads my way. "They filled my locker with the trash from the dumpster. Discarded cafeteria food." She blinks away tears.

I say the first thing that comes to mind. "You need to get your combination changed. You know they won't stop at this."

She nods. "I can't believe I used to be friends with them. I knew they could be mean, but I never thought they'd turn on me. All the times we hung out together. That should count for something."

"They're bullies. And they get away with it because no one stands up to them."

Kendra kicks at the floor. "I know. I can't believe I was ever part of it."

Thorn volunteers to go to the office to ask the janitor to clean out Kendra's locker. She and I head to class at his insistence, but I don't think this is the end of it. If they've targeted Kendra, she's in for a tough time.

We start down the hall side by side. Kendra stops and faces me. "I envy you, you know."

My mouth drops open. "What? Me? Why would you envy me?"

Kendra kicks at the floor. "You don't care what anyone thinks. You do your own thing."

I huff air through my nose. "There is no 'my own thing' for me. I'm a mess. I barely get through the day. Running is the only thing that keeps me going. You've got everything going for you. Two parents. A nice house. A safe neighborhood."

She sighs. "Two parents who work all the time because they want to buy more and more. The newest and best of everything to stay a step ahead of their friends. I'm happy enough with what we have. I'd rather have them home." She pauses and stares at the floor. "And the two people who used to be my best friends filled my locker with trash. I know they'll sabotage me any way they can."

"Ignore them. Besides, you probably know some secrets they wouldn't want broadcast around school."

She grins and claps her hands together. "You're right. I do."

The warning bell rings before I can ask her about it, and we hurry to class. I drop into my seat, but my mind is processing. Someone envies me? That's a first. I smile.

The mood is different at track today. From the moment we arrive, it's all business.

"We have three days to practice, and then, we have our first meet." Coach Jones crosses his arms and walks the length of the bleachers, not looking at any of us. He walks halfway back, then turns and faces us. "Some of you have no track background, so I'm counting especially on the returning track team members this first meet. We'll all work hard the next three days, and we'll give a hundred and ten percent. We'll run our fastest, jump our highest, and do it with a good attitude."

He lifts a hand and rubs his chin as he looks across the bleachers. He turns to Coach Clark. "You want to take the ones you think would do best in the field events, and I'll work with the others?"

She glances across the bleachers, a frown on her face. "I'll take girls for the high jump, long jump, and triple jump."

I get up and start down the bleachers. Coach Clark looks at me, and I meet her gaze. She turns to Coach Jones. "I think Scott would be best on relays. Or maybe the one- or two-mile."

Coach Jones turns to me. "You want to run in the 4x400?

4x800? We can use another strong runner."

I swallow. "I thought I could do high jump and long jump."

Coach Clark shakes her head. "Maybe next year. I have enough high jumpers from last year."

Heat rushes up my neck and across my face. I've been the second highest jumper in practice, but she's excluding me? I've never done anything to her. Coach Jones is watching me, smiling. No clue anything is wrong. "Come on, relay isn't hard to learn. With your speed, you'll be an asset on the relays. In a 4x400, four girls each run 400 meters—one full lap. It goes fast. A 4x800 is the same except that you run two full laps. After you run, you hand off the baton to the next runner."

I nod. Relay it is. Besides, I'd rather work with Coach Jones than Coach Clark any day. I just wonder why she suddenly doesn't want me on high jump. Does it have to do with finding out who my mom is?

After we're warmed up and stretched, Coach Jones calls us together. Three of the high jumpers are also in relay—Michaela, Sasha and Katelyn. They seem to be the ones who hold the team together. Jordyn too. Instead of going to high jump, they stay to work with relay.

He glances across the girls in front of him. "Michaela, Jordyn, Megan, Paige, team one. Sasha, Kendra, Kiana, Katelyn, team two. Running a 4x400. Let's keep the speed up and get that baton passed off without losing any time."

The relay is close with Michaela leading off for one team and Sasha for the other. The two teams are within seconds of each other all the way around. In the final turn, Paige leans forward and sprints past Katelyn, finishing two seconds ahead.

"Good job!" Coach Jones says. I know he's not talking to me personally, but neither is he criticizing me. "Line up again and let's go for the 4x800."

Our take offs and baton passes are smoother, and it feels like it's coming together well. Working with Coach Jones is easier than with Coach Clark. He works us hard, but always has a smile on his face and an encouraging word. I haven't heard Coach Clark say a good word to anyone except Sasha, Michaela, and Jordyn. She definitely doesn't have a good word to say about our head coach. What could have happened to cause the tension between them? Since Coach Jones hasn't been back to our town since high school, whatever it was must have been from when they were both track stars here.

I turn my attention back to practice and gear up for the next event. I need to focus all my energy on getting ready for the meet. Still, I can't help but wonder.

Tuesday practice is easier. After practice, Coach approaches me. "Coming to the church later?"

"If you want me to."

"I'd like to have you there. The freerun club hasn't been officially approved, but we can work on some moves in the gym—and play some basketball to keep the guys happy."

Thorn and I have been busy doing homework and lawn work, being at the house as little as possible. I've successfully avoided spending any time with my grandfather. I want to help Thorn this afternoon, but he says there's nothing for me to do at this job. He drops me off at the house, promising to be back as soon as he can.

No one is home when I go inside, so I microwave a frozen dinner, then jog the three miles to the church. The little ones are painting with watercolors at tables set up in one half of the gym. I'm earlier than usual, and there's no sign of Coach. Carolyn and a younger woman are with the children. A young boy with milk chocolate skin and tight, curly hair looks at me and smiles. I walk over to him. He holds up a picture. "Look, I painted my dog."

I smile. "That's nice. What's his name?"

"Boxer," he replies, "and my name is Malakai."

I look around at the tables. Isabella isn't seated at any of them. "Didn't Isabella come today?"

Malakai makes another brushstroke. "She came."

I scan the tables again more carefully. "I don't see her."

Malakai looks up from his painting. "She spilled paint on her shirt, and the man said he'd help her wipe it off."

"What man?"

Malakai adds a sun to his picture. "The old man that's here when we get here after school."

My grandfather? My gut says yes.

Malakai dips his paint in green and trails it across the bottom of his paper. "Look! Grass."

"Nice grass." I touch his arm. He looks up at me. "Malakai, this is really important. Where did the man take Isabella?"

"Back there." He points down the hallway. "To the restroom."

My breathing quickens. I take a deep breath and force myself to release it slowly. He doesn't need to know I'm upset. "Thank you, Malakai. I think I'll go check on them."

I turn and hurry across the gym to the hallway. The lights are on, but the hallway is still shadowy. I trot toward the restrooms and stop outside the girls' restroom. I push the door open. It's empty. I step to the boys' restroom and listen. There's a low murmur of voices. Then the sound of the hand dryer erases the quietness. I crack the door open. Isabella has her back to me. She's wearing only jeans and tennis shoes. My grandfather is drying her shirt in front of the dryer.

I step inside. "What are you doing?"

My grandfather looks up. He smiles. "Isabella spilled her paint. She was afraid her mother would be angry if she came home with a dirty shirt."

Isabella looks at me with wide brown eyes. "He fixed it for me. Now I won't get into trouble."

Thoughts spin in my mind. She thinks he's a hero. I know better. Still, she seems fine. "Why don't you get your shirt back on so you can go back to your friends. Don't you want to paint a picture for your mother?"

I snatch the shirt from my grandfather and help her back into it. Isabella looks up at me. "I want to paint a picture for him. He's my friend now." She turns and smiles at my grandfather. I clench my teeth. She's too young to understand.

We walk back into the gym. Carolyn is collecting the paint and brushes. The three of us walk over. "He had her alone in the guys' bathroom," I tell Carolyn. Surely, she will see a problem with that. Carolyn looks from me to my grandfather.

My grandfather smiles at Carolyn. He motions to Isabella. "She spilled paint on herself. She's all cleaned up now."

Carolyn frowns. "You shouldn't have taken her back there by yourself. Only leaders of the same sex may take children to the restroom, and even then, the door should be left open."

My grandfather gives her an apologetic smile. "She was distraught. I just wanted to help her out."

"Well, no harm done this time, but you must follow the safety rules," Carolyn says.

My grandfather smiles his most charming smile at her. "But of course."

I open my mouth to say something, then clamp it shut.

Carolyn turns to me. "Do you have something more to say? It seems to me that you're overly concerned about Mr. Scott."

My grandfather smiles. "Oh, she's my granddaughter. I think she just likes to be with me."

Carolyn looks at me and then at him. She makes a sound of displeasure, turns, and walks to the children.

I walk back into the now empty gym and grab a basketball from the rack. Might as well take my frustrations out on the ball.

Movement catches my eye. Coach Jones enters the gym, and my spirits lift. He sees me and jogs over. He snatches the basketball from me, shoots it at the basket, and it swishes in.

Coach then pushes a large foam square near the middle of a mat. "Help me set up the blocks to demonstrate some vaults?"

I join him, and we prepare the gym for the older kids. We're just finishing when a group arrives, pushing each other and teasing one of the boys about a girl he likes. They grab a basketball from the rack and start playing two on two until Coach calls them to the bleachers.

"This evening we are going to work on a couple of different vaults. We'll start with the side vault we showed you last time. Kia will demonstrate, and then you can line up and give it a go."

I run at the first block and execute a perfect side vault. Then I continue around the gym doing it on the rectangles and squares we placed. Eighteen boys and three girls attempt to copy me. Some of them are good, while others miss. Coach demonstrates the vault again. His vaults are both powerful and graceful. Like Thorn's.

We teach them the dash vault, and then Coach lets them play basketball. For that amount of time, I forget about my grandfather. But as soon as I'm at home in my room, questions consume my thoughts. Questions that don't have easy answers.

Chapter Eleven

Thursday dawns as a beautiful day. Our high school is hosting the first track meet of the season. The down side is that Thorn's grandparents are coming home today, and Mom has said it's time for me to face things. She believes Grandpa has proven to be a different person, so starting tonight, I'm on my own. No Thorn. No staying with his grandparents.

I shut that out of my mind and focus on the upcoming meet. The track team is dismissed right after lunch. Coach has posted a list of the track team members and what event each is running. I scan it and find my name for the 4x800 relay and the 3200-meter. The 4x800 is the first event of the day, but the 3200-meter run is near the end.

After Coach Jones hands out royal blue uniforms with gold stripes, our school colors, we head for the locker room. The girls who were on the team last year joke with each other as they quickly dress. Nervousness fills my stomach.

I inspect my uniform. It's not new. Someone else had number 17 last year. But it's the first time I've ever worn a team uniform. Jordyn glances my way. "Cool. You have Latavia's uniform. She was the best sprinter last year and got a scholarship to Alabama. Maybe the uniform will bring you luck."

I grin. "Hope so."

"Starting with the next meet, you'll get to wear the blue and gold warm-up suit to school on game day," Jordyn tells me.

We walk out of the locker room as a team. The boys' team has emerged ahead of us, Thorn among them. He is standing in a group joking around. How can they be so relaxed?

Four other teams arrive from nearby high schools for the opening meet, and the excitement mounts. Kendra walks up to me. "Ready?"

"I guess." My nervousness keeps me from saying more.

Coach puts us through warm-ups, and my nerves calm as I feel the ground beneath my pounding feet. The sound system turns on with a squeal that startles everyone, and the announcer comes on the PA system to welcome the teams and call the participants to the start areas for the first four events. I turn and head to the field to find the other team members.

Katelyn Harmon jogs up to us. "There are some girls here who are really fast." She points to a tall, African-American girl. "That's Shondra from Central. She's crazy fast in sprints and relays."

I look at the runner. "She must be six feet tall!"

Katelyn laughs. "She's pretty close, so it's hard to keep up with her. See the red-haired twins over there?"

I look over at them. "They look friendly."

"They are. But they are also really fast. Holly and Lauren. They run for Holy Nativity. You'll get to know a lot of the girls from other schools from seeing them at all the meets. Most are nice, but some are overly competitive, though."

It's almost time for Kendra, Jordyn, Sasha, and me to run the 4x800 when Kendra tenses as she looks toward the bleachers. Leila and Zoey are there. A thin, blond girl is with them. I turn to Kendra. "Who's that?"

"Brittany. She was our friend in middle school, but she goes to the charter high school. We lost touch with her."

"Why is she here today? We're not running against her school."

Kendra scowls. "She's here with Leila and Zoey so all three can laugh if we mess up."

I clench my teeth. "Then we won't mess up."

She nods, and we take our place on the track. Jordyn leads off for our team. She's out front most of her two laps. She finishes in 2:40.8 and slaps the baton in my hand. The 4x800 is all about pacing, and I keep my cadence steady, focusing on Kendra, who is running after me. I enter the changeover zone and slap the baton neatly in her hand, and she's off. I hope Kendra does well, knowing Leila and her crew are eager for her to fail. She completes her split in 2:50.10. Sasha, at anchor, quickly closes the distance between herself and the opponent in front of her. The other runner puts on a burst of speed in the final stretch, but Sasha has some fire left too and regains the lead as they cross the finish line.

We finish at 10:33.29. First in our heat, but second overall. I grin and high five my teammates. I don't run the 3200 until later, so I wander over to where some of the girls are gathered to cheer for the other events.

Coach Clark calls the girls for the 100-meter hurdles, then Coach Jones calls the girls for the 100-meter sprint. We watch as Sasha and Michaela take the first two places in the sprint for our school. Katelyn Harmon isn't far behind.

The 1600-meter run, Kendra's next event, follows the sprint. As she takes her place on the start line for the 1600, a voice calls out, "Don't trip." I turn toward the stands. Leila, Zoey and Brittany are smirking. Why did I look?

I ignore them, joining some of the other girls at the sidelines to cheer for our teammates. "Let's go, Kendra," I yell.

Kendra is running against Shondra, the tall runner from Central that Katelyn pointed out to me. It's a tight race on the track for the 1600-meter. Kendra isn't pacing well. She can run faster. I've seen it. But now she's near the back for this heat. Toward the end, she speeds up to pass the girl in front of her, but still ends with a below-average time of 6:56.

Coach Clark comes over from the field area in time to see Kendra's finish. She calls her over. Coach is right in Kendra's face. I take a step toward them, then stop. I don't want to make things worse with Coach Clark. Kendra can hold her own.

Thorn takes his place on the start line for the boys' 1600, his first event. He looks confident, and when the start gun sounds, he starts out strong leading the way. He's not as tall as many of the runners, but he's as fast. He comes down the first stretch by me. I yell, "Go Thorn!"

Concentration is etched on his face. This is serious for him. Thorn is passing me again. How fast is he running? Four laps around and I have the answer when he hits the finish line at 5:22.10. He stops at the team cooler for a drink, then heads over to talk to us.

"Thorn, that was amazing!"

He lifts an eyebrow at me. I playfully punch his arm. "Stop it. Today you ran even faster than in tryouts."

"I didn't expect to be under six minutes. It just came together for me."

His coach calls, and he runs to join his teammates.

Jordyn gives me a funny look.

"What?" I ask.

"He's kind of cute."

Blush rolls up my neck. "It's not like that."

"Why not?"

I hesitate. "I guess we've been friends for so long. I've never thought of him any other way."

Jordyn grins. "You might want to give it some thought." She turns back to the track. The conversation raises questions in my mind, but I shut them out. I don't want things to change between Thorn and me—at least not yet.

I cheer as event after event is run. Then the 3200 is called. It's going to be a tough race, but at least I'm not running against Shondra. Still, the other girls look fast. I need to focus and pace myself. I take off with the start gun and let my mind clear as I make my way around the track eight times. I cross the line at 12:13.38. It's a good time for me, and I'm second in the heat, but only fourth overall.

I glance toward the stands to see if Leila and Zoey are watching. Heat rushes through me like a hurricane. My grandfather is here! Not only that, but he's sitting by Leila, Zoey and Brittany, engaging them in conversation. What is he doing here? How did he know about the meet? Then, I realize he must have seen the schedule I fastened on the refrigerator. That answers the how did he know question, but not the why. As much as my mother wants to believe it, he hasn't suddenly become the dad she always wanted or the grandfather she wants for me.

I don't realize I'm staring until Leila turns and winks at me, then links her arm through my grandfather's. What is she playing at? If she had any clue! Of course, she's safe, and I guess I should be glad he's here, not with Isabella at the center, but still ...

I tear my gaze away and go to join my team, pretending not to see my grandfather or to know who he is.

The events finish, and I glance at the bleachers. Empty. Even the three girls are gone. I take my place by the other girls at the awards ceremony to accept my second-place ribbon for the 4x800 and my fourth place for the 3200-meter. Some girls placed in all four of their events, the maximum number of events you can enter. Thorn receives three ribbons—third for the 1600m, third in high jump, and fourth in triple jump.

After the meet, Thorn drives me home. He glances over at me. "You did good for your first meet."

I hold up my ribbons. "First two ribbons. Of course, Sasha and Jordyn carried the 4x800."

Thorn scowls. "Don't underestimate yourself. You held your own on your leg of the relay."

"Maybe. But you flew on the 1600. You'll be the one to get a scholarship to college for track."

Thorn is silent.

"What?"

"I haven't really thought that far ahead. I guess I see myself working for my grandfather."

"He can hire someone else. I'm sure he'd want you to go to college, even if it's community college."

"But he always talks about me taking over, so he can work part-time or retire."

I frown. "So get a business degree first— if that's what you really want. Remember what you told me? Run toward who you're meant to be? That's true for you too."

Thorn's hands grip the steering tighter, and his lips tighten. Have I angered him?

He clears his throat. "I don't know how that works for me."

I sigh. "Me either." I hold up the ribbons. "But this is a start."

When I arrive home, I head to my room and try to concentrate on my homework. I can hear the low murmur of voices from the television below. Mom will be glued to the show for the next hour. I can't focus on the words on the page in front of me. I stand and pace my room. It figures the church people would love my grandfather—a nice older man to be grandfather to the little kids and part of the senior citizens group. Am I wrong about him? Has he really changed? My gut says no.

The door to Mom's bedroom is open. It's his bedroom now. I hesitate in the doorway. What did he bring with him? He'd already unpacked by the time I got home that day. I glance around but don't see much of anything. Curiosity gets the best of me.

I step inside and flip the light switch. The bulb illuminates the room. There's a hint of fragrance lingering in the air—like expensive men's aftershave. But it doesn't cover the smell of the mildew clinging to the walls.

I glance around. Not much has changed. There's a man's long-sleeved button-up shirt thrown on the bed and a stack of private detective books on the bedside stand. I pick up the top one and flip through it. I never took him for a reader.

I take a hesitant step toward the closet. I reach out, grab the handle, and start to ease it open. It lets out a squeak. I freeze and listen. Nothing. I ease it farther open and look in. Mom's clothes hang on half the rod. A few men's shirts hang on the other. Where are his belongings? His clothes? If he plans to stay until he dies, wouldn't he have brought everything with him?

I back out of the closet and shut the door as quietly as possible, but the squeak sounds loud in my ears. I listen. There's only the murmur of the television set in the living room. I turn and look around. The worn chenille bedspread is caught up on one side. I walk to the bed and reach to straighten the bedspread. The top mattress isn't lying flat. I slip my hand between mattresses to find out why, and my hand hits something hard. The back of my neck prickles.

My hand closes around the object, and I pull out an electronic tablet. Thorn's grandfather has one for work, but I didn't know my grandfather had one. Why is his hidden between mattresses?

I push the power button and the tablet comes on. I slide my finger across the screen, and it opens to a list of files. He hasn't put a password on it? Probably doesn't think he needs it. I click on the photo gallery. It opens to the photo of a young girl smiling at the camera. She looks familiar, but my mom is an only child, so he doesn't have any other grandchildren or great grandchildren. Who is she?

I scroll through picture after picture of young, smiling girls. Then I catch my breath. I'm looking at a picture of Isabella in the bathroom with her shirt off. I hadn't noticed him holding a tablet when I found him with her. Are these pictures of the girls in the after-school program at the church? Maybe that's why the one looked familiar. I might have seen her leaving the church.

Headlights sweep across the house, catching my attention. I glance out the window. My grandfather has turned into the driveway. Why is he back? Does he see his room light is on?

I shove the tablet between the mattresses, turn out the light and hurry to my own room. I shut my door and sit on my bed, leaning against the pillows, history book on my lap, as the front door opens. Suddenly I freeze, a chill squeezing at my chest, as I realize I left Grandpa's tablet on! Even if it hibernates, it'll still be open to the photo gallery.

I have to turn it off. Standing, I take a step toward my door. A board creaks under my foot, sounding like a shot in the silence. Did he hear that? Where is he? I take another step. I'm trying to walk silently, but the floor isn't cooperating. I slowly ease my door open.

A footstep sounds on the bottom stair.

"Forgot something I need for tonight," my grandfather calls out, presumably to my mom in the living room.

I don't have time to make it to his room and back. I quietly close my door and turn the lock, then ease back onto my bed, lying back against my pillow. How could I have been so careless to forget to turn the tablet off? Maybe he'll think he left it open to the pictures.

I'm silent as my grandfather goes into his room. He's only there for a minute, then footsteps sound on the stairs again. He's leaving. As he backs his car out, his headlights cut an arc across the house. I open my door, quickly cross the hall, and enter his room. Reaching between the mattresses, I feel for the tablet. It's gone! Heaviness pushes in on me. Will he know the pictures have been looked at?

Chapter Twelve

The next morning, I am at the curb, bouncing on the balls of my feet. I reach in my pocket and wrap my hand around my Statue of Liberty souvenir coin, rubbing it between my thumb and first two fingers as I watch for Thorn's truck. I hear the rumble of the engine. He pulls up, and I quickly jump in.

Thorn looks at me. "What's up? You look pretty ... anxious."

I lean back against the seat and catch my breath, then I tell him about the tablet.

He grips the steering wheel. "Just regular photos?"

"Yeah, except the ones of Isabella with her shirt off. But even without that one, don't you think it's a little weird that he has a whole gallery of photos of young girls?"

Thorn's brows lower. "Maybe he took them for the church. Like to put on the wall or something."

"Then why aren't there pictures of the boys? And what about the shirtless ones?"

Thorn taps his fingers on his steering wheel as he waits for a light. "Don't know. Sounds suspicious, but not enough to tell anyone about. You tell your mom about it?"

"She's too busy pretending everything is okay—that her father has changed and this is a regular family visit. Besides, he'll have an explanation for the pictures just like he did for taking Isabella into the restroom. Come with me to the church this afternoon?"

Thorn agrees.

After school, we drive to his house first to finish up a little homework and let his grandparents know where he's going before we leave. I text Mom. It's Friday, so she'll go out drinking with her friends unless she's doing something with her dad.

We walk to Thorn's truck. He pulls out and turns toward the church. "Is your dad better?"

"Not really. Still unconscious. Don't know why we have to go visit when he won't know whether we're there or not." Frustration tinges Thorn's words.

"They say that sometimes people hear other people talking to them even when they're unconscious." My words sound hollow even to me.

"That's what Grandma says. She wants to read the Bible to him and pray over him. Says we'll pray for a healed body and heart."

"She believes he's changed?"

"She wants to believe he's changed, that his talk about God and salvation is real. But I think it's hard for any of us to believe it after all that's happened in the past. But it's not just that."

I wait. Finally, I ask, "What?"

"They think everything will be different when he wakes up, but there's not going to be some storybook happy ending."

No wise words come to mind, so I reach out and squeeze his fingers. We arrive at the church as the younger children are leaving and some of the older ones are arriving. Many of them are on foot or riding bikes with torn seats and worn tires. I understand. Everything I have is second-hand and well-worn. I don't even have a bike since I outgrew the twenty-inch bike I rode to school in my elementary years.

Isabella is walking out of the church. She sees me and smiles. "I remember you. You were there when the nice man fixed my shirt. What's your name? And who is that?" She points at Thorn.

I force myself to smile, not because she's done anything wrong, but because of the reminder of my grandfather breaking the rules. "Hi, Isabella. My name is Kiana. This is my friend Thorn."

I catch sight of my grandfather. He's looking our way. The question is—who is he watching, me or Isabella?

Isabella beams at Thorn, and he smiles in return. She looks toward the road. "My mommy is here. I gotta go." Skipping down the sidewalk, she climbs into a car, and her mother pulls away.

More of the middle school kids are arriving, so we go into the gym. Carolyn is still there with a few younger children whose parents haven't yet signed them out. She frowns when she sees me and ignores Thorn altogether.

"Friendly," he mutters under his breath.

Thorn and I get a basketball and take turns shooting until Coach arrives and calls the group to the bleachers. He gestures toward Thorn. "This is Thorn. He will be helping with the freerunning club I'm trying to start."

Chance jumps up. "You got any better moves than the girl?"

Coach Jones crosses his arms over his chest. "Sit down, Chance. What did I say about showing respect? You want to run laps?"

Chance sits, and Coach turns to Thorn. "You want to show them some freerunning?"

"Sure." Thorn glances around, surveying the gym. He turns to me. "Help me set up?"

I nod and help move the mats.

Lips tight and eyes focused, Thorn sprints toward two large, square mats. He builds speed as he leaps lands with his hands at the front of the mat. It looks like he's going to do a kong vault where he would bring his knees between his hands, but instead he only brings them partway, then inverts his body, holding his feet up in the air similar to a handstand. He uses his momentum to dive into a second kong vault like he's playing leapfrog. He keeps his knees to his chest as his legs swing between his arms and out in front of him. He clears the mat and lands on the floor.

I hear the intake of breath and glance behind me. All eyes are focused on Thorn. Even the boys are mesmerized by his skill.

Thorn circles around and lands on top of the mats again, this time balancing on his hands, legs in the air as he spins in a circle on his hands. He flips off the mat, landing on his feet then sprints full speed at a wall. Gasps fill the air as Thorn runs about eight feet up, then flips straight back and goes into a series of three back flips on the floor. I glance at Chance. He's hooked, his eyes riveted on Thorn.

Thorn runs up the wall again and side flips twice before landing, then finishes with a series of cartwheels that lands him in front of the bleachers.

Coach has the kids watch as he demonstrates in slow motion some of the moves Thorn just finished doing. Then we work with the kids on learning the skills.

After Coach gives another talk about trusting God and the last middle school student leaves, Coach turns to us. "I'm going to try to create a freerunning routine in the courtyard at the school. Want to come along?"

I look at Thorn. He turns to Coach. "We'll follow you."

Thorn follows Coach, then pulls into the parking lot beside him.

The fence around the school courtyard is locked since it's after hours. Coach unlocks it, then turns on the courtyard lights.

Several picnic tables and benches dot the area around a rock garden. A flagpole stands like a sentinel in the middle of the garden, surrounded by a low stone wall. On the other side of the wall are bikes racks and a ramp with handrails for handicapped students. A cement wall surrounds an air-conditioning unit.

"You said you're creating a freerunning routine?" Thorn asks.

"One of the perks of winning *Running Free*. A company hired me to make a freerunning commercial to advertise their line of sports clothing."

"Wow! That is so cool!" I'm gushing like Leila, so I clamp my lips shut.

Coach rubs his chin with one hand. "I need to put some moves together. That's where you two can help me. This is what I have to work with—picnic tables, flagpole, handrails, cement walls. What do you think?"

Thorn surveys the area, then, without saying a word, he takes off running. Coach follows him while I stand and watch. They sprint, Coach following Thorn, toward the picnic tables. Thorn reaches the first one, tucks his legs close to his chest and pushes off from his fingertips to clear it without clipping his feet. He reaches the second picnic table, jumping toward it feet first with his legs outstretched and pushing with his hands as he crosses it. Coach follows, his muscles rippling as he clears the picnic table.

Thorn lands and does front flips to the pole where he spins and uses the momentum to do a cat grab on the tall wall, gripping the top with his fingers. He wall-climbs, stopping on top, where Coach joins him. I'm mesmerized. It's like watching a dance—a dance with cool moves.

With ninja-like agility, they side-flip off the wall, landing with perfect precision on the garden border below. Thorn turns and does a wall-climb back to the top of the wall and walks the length of it on his hands. Coach copies him. Reaching the end, they both back-flip off, landing on the balls of their feet before going into a series of back flips on the ground, their shoulder muscles defined under their tank tops.

Thorn turns to Coach. "Something like that?"

Coach grins. "I think they have the wrong person doing the video."

Thorn shrugs one shoulder. "Grew up with this. Kia's not bad either. She's just newer to it."

"I need to put it to music," Coach says. He pulls out his iPod, starts a song, and then takes off. Thorn and I perch on top a picnic table to watch. Coach wall-climbs, shoulder muscles taut, stands, and back flips the length of the wall, dismounting with a side flip. He mounts the handrail on the ramp leading to the building and runs up, his feet sure on the narrow surface.

"Not bad," Thorn says.

I nod. The music accentuates Coach's strength and agility.

Coach front-flips from the handrail and sprints toward the wall, where he plants his left foot hip high, then brings the other knee up and starts his rotation. He drops his head back and brings both legs together as he flips over backward and nails a perfect wall flip. He works the wall, pole, rails, and picnic benches to the music. When the song ends, he jogs over to us.

My mouth is hanging open. "Whoa. You're like a professional."

Coach grins. "I learned on the streets of Miami." He sits on top of the other picnic table facing me.

"You grew up in Miami?" I ask.

Coach clasps his hands together and studies them. "I grew up there, and I grew up here." He studies his hands, then looks up at us. "My older brother and I were born near Miami. My dad was a preacher. Mom stayed home to take care of us. That might sound like an ideal life, but it wasn't. We were preacher's kids, so we had to be the example."

He stops and looks out into the darkness, then continues. "My older brother rebelled and got into a gang and into drugs. I don't know how long it went on—two, three years maybe. My dad tried to get him out of it, but all it did was get my dad shot and killed by a drug dealer. On top of that, my brother Gerald got sent to prison."

Thorn and I sit silently, waiting for Coach to continue. His eyes are looking into the past. Finally, he speaks. "It was just Mom and me then. Right before my sophomore year of high school, Mom moved us up here to the panhandle to get me away from the drugs and gangs. She has a sister here. I lived here until the day after high school graduation, then I left."

He meets my gaze. "I didn't do drugs, but I wasn't the model teen either. God had let my dad get killed and my brother go to prison, so I didn't have much use for him. Through it all, Mom was always there for me, believing in me despite all. She's the reason I went to college and then tried out for *Running Free*."

"But if you moved to the panhandle, why did you say you were from Miami on *Running Free*?" Thorn questions.

"I went back to Miami for college, and then, I taught in a middle school there for several years before trying out for the show. I thought if I could reach the young kids, I could keep them off drugs. And maybe for a few, I made a difference. But after the show, I was ready for a change. I decided to come back up here and be near my mom."

"So, you knew Coach Clark from high school?" I blurt out.

Coach looks at me, and I bite at my bottom lip.

"I do. We both ran track for South Bay."

"She doesn't seem like much of a ... fan," I say.

He rubs his hands down his shorts. "That is a true statement. We have a lot of history. You know how it is in high school."

I do know. I want to ask more, but it would be rude, so I stay silent.

"The thing is, I know that in everything that happened, God was there, and he was working."

"Even with your dad getting killed? How was that God working? Why didn't he stop it from happening?" The words rush from my mouth before I know I'm going to say them.

"I won't even pretend to understand God's ways," Coach says. "But it brought me and my mom closer, and it led to me learning to freerun. I was angry when Dad died and Gerald went to prison, and I needed a safe way to work through the anger, so I started hanging out at the park where kids did freerunning. Later in college, I got into a Christian freerunning group, and I regained my belief in God."

I should say something, but I don't know what to say, so I don't say anything. Neither does Thorn, who is glancing sideways at me. Coach seems to understand. He puts a hand on my shoulder. "God has a plan, and sometimes bad stuff happens. We don't always know why, but he can use even the bad stuff to do something good."

Coach looks at his watch. "It's getting late. We'd better go." He walks Thorn and me to the truck, then heads to his car.

Thorn drops me off at my house. I notice the light is on in my grandfather's room, so I enter through the back door. Mom looks up from her television show long enough to acknowledge me.

I climb the stairs as quietly as possible, hoping not to disturb my grandfather. Step to the right on the second step and to the left on the sixth step. Skip the seventh step altogether. I'm stepping over the next to the top step when I see a movement in the hall. My foot comes down, and the step lets out an aching groan.

My grandfather is standing in the door of his room, tablet in hand. He watches me, a smirk on his face, as I scurry into my room and close the door. Now I know how a mouse must feel right before it's swallowed by a snake.

Chapter Thirteen

Saturday dawns bright with cool weather, perfect for a track meet. Holy Nativity is hosting it, so we load the bus for the half-hour trip, then warm up at their track. The same teams we ran against last week are here, but there are also two schools here that weren't at the first meet because this is a bigger meet. I watch the other competitors warm up, trying to evaluate their strengths.

Shondra from Central is here. I turn to Kendra with a groan. "I hope I don't have to run against her. Look, the red-haired twins from Holy Nativity are here too. Those are the only ones I know by name."

Kendra looks around. "Me too. Doesn't it feel funny to know the names of the competitors? Do you think we'll all be friends by the end of the season?"

"With some of them maybe." I survey the area. "Some look friendlier than others."

"Are you ready for the 4x800? It's our first event."

I nod. "I think so."

I glance toward the bleachers. "Oh great. Leila, Zoey, and Brittany are here again. Are they going to come to every meet and hope for us to mess up?"

Kendra's lips tighten. "They're probably interested in someone on the boys' team."

We stroll to the track and wait for the event to be called, then take our place on the track. We're running it in the same order as the first meet, so when the gun fires, Jordyn takes off. She soon passes the others and holds first place completing her lap in 2:32.30. She slaps the baton into my hand, but I hesitate before I close my hand around it. I fumble the baton, breaking my concentration. I get a slow start and fight to find my stride. I sprint, trying to catch up with the runner from Holy Nativity who's right ahead of me. I pass her, but I'm still too slow. My leg of the race is 2:52.30, twenty seconds slower than Jordyn. It's going to be up to Kendra and Sasha to make up the time.

In my eagerness to get the baton to Kendra, I try to slap it into her hand too soon. It hits the ground and bounces. Kendra snatches it and sprints, but we're too far behind. Legs pumping, Kendra pushes the whole way, but finishes last. Sasha is our only hope, but even she can't pull it off. She makes up time, passing Central and Northeast, but we finish sixth out of eight teams.

Coach Jones is at the finish line. He taps me on the shoulder. "Stuff like that happens. We'll do better next time."

Coach Clark doesn't say anything, but her nose is wrinkled as though she smells something bad as she observes me through narrowed eyes. I turn and walk toward the rest of our team. Leila, Zoey, and Brittany are coming my way. Leila smirks. "Good job. You lost that for the team. Guess Coach Clark threw the wrong people off the team."

I mentally count to ten, then look Leila in the eyes. "Wow. I'm touched you cared enough about us to come to an away meet." Before she can answer, I turn and stride away.

Kendra falls in step beside me and hands me a blue raspberry sports drink. "What did you say to them?"

I crack the lid of the sports drink and take a sip. "Nothing much, why?"

"You should have seen the look on Leila's face. Wish I'd gotten a picture. It was priceless."

I turn to Kendra. "She said I lost the relay for our team, and she was right. I messed up the pass. I ran too slow. I did everything wrong."

She stops walking. "It happens. It's our first year."

I try to smile, but it falls flat. "Thanks, even if you're only saying that to make me feel better."

I stand on the sidelines and cheer for my teammates and for the boys' team too. Thorn is even faster on the 1600 than the last meet.

The 3200-meter is announced, and I jog to the track. I take my place at the start line, Shondra on one side and a red-haired twin on the other. I'm going to have to push the whole way to beat any of their times. The gun signals the start of the race, and we're off. I try to pace with Shondra, but it takes two of my strides to match one of hers, so I pace with a runner from Northeast who's a bit faster than I am, matching her stride for stride, but push myself to pass her in the last lap.

I finish strong at 12.14.64 and take fourth place in our heat. It's a good start, but I'm going to have to do better if I want to go to districts.

When our bus arrives back at school, Thorn and I quickly head for his truck. I lean my head back against the seat and close my eyes.

"It wasn't that bad," Thorn said.

"So Coach Jones says, but did you see the look Coach Clark gave me?"

"You care why?" Thorn asks.

"Don't know. Guess I don't want to give her more of a reason to be out to get me."

"You really think she's out to get you?"

I open my eyes and sit up. "Well, something's going on. Right after she asks me if Melonie Scott is my mom, she removes me from the high jump and long jump. You think that's a coincidence?"

"Maybe she had enough jumpers and thought you'd be better at relays."

"I was second to Sasha every time."

Thorn pulls to the curb. "Don't know. Wouldn't let it get to you though. Just focus on the events you have this year."

I climb out and head into the house, not sure what to expect.

Mom is sitting on the couch watching television. She picks up the remote and clicks off the show when I walk in. "How's track going?"

I stop. "You really want to know how track is going?"

"I wouldn't have asked if I didn't."

"You've never asked before."

She frowns. "It's not that I don't care. I just get too caught up in my own world."

Well, at least she's honest tonight.

Mom walks to the kitchen and grabs a beer from the refrigerator. After cracking the top and taking a sip, she asks, "Are you enjoying track?"

"Except for Coach Clark. She seems to dislike me, and I have no clue why."

"It probably just seems that way."

"I don't think so. She was at South Bay the same time you were. Cassandra Clark?"

Mom's eyes widen. "Cassandra Clark? She's your coach?"

"So you do know her?"

"Oh, yeah, I know her all right. You get on her bad side, you may as well forget track. She can hold a grudge forever."

My mind spins. "Are you talking about yourself or someone else?"

Mom nibbles at her bottom lip. "Both, I guess."

I study her. "What did you do?"

"Oh, it was a guy thing. You know how that is."

"Not first-hand. But I see it. The break-up drama, that is. You didn't steal her guy or anything, did you?"

Mom shrugs one shoulder. "It was a long time ago. I didn't think she even knew he liked me."

"Why wouldn't she know?"

She sighs. "It was complicated." Mom's lips tighten, and her eyes go dark. She's done talking for now.

"If you ever want to come to a meet, my schedule is on the fridge." I think about telling her that her father was at my meet, but to her it'll just be another reassurance he wants to be part of the family—that he's trying to support me.

As I head upstairs, I can't help but wonder: Would Coach Clark really hold such a grudge against Mom all these years that she doesn't want Melonie Scott's daughter on her team?

Chapter Fourteen

Track practice gets tougher as we progress further into the season. Coach Clark gets less tolerant with each meet even though we place well. She wants to be coach of the number one team, and we aren't giving her that. Track is still a big part of my week, but more and more I look forward to Tuesdays and Fridays when I'm helping with the middle school kids at the church. At least they don't make me feel a complete failure.

With six meets behind us, we are just days away from the county meet. The girls' team is in good standing, but you wouldn't know it by Coach Clark's moods.

"County meet is this Friday and Saturday. Do you understand that?" She paces up and down by the bleachers. "If you can't jump higher, run faster than this, we may as well stay home. Do you hear me?" She looks up into the bleachers. I look down, not wanting to meet her eyes.

"Coach Jones is with the boys' team today, so we'll warm up with a mile run, then stretch out. Sasha, you lead. Then everyone to the high jump pit. It won't hurt anyone to give it a try. The majority of our long jumpers and high jumpers are seniors, so they won't be back next year. Some of you will need to take their places."

After warming up, I line up with the other girls for high jump. When I reach the front of the line, I take off strong and do a J curve as I approach the bar. I turn my body, bringing my knee up, and go backwards over the bar. I clip the bar with my foot, knocking it off.

Coach Clark glares. "What was that? I thought you wanted to be a high jumper?"

I bite back a retort and head to the back of the line.

She follows. "I was talking to you. You don't walk away from me."

My ears grow warm as I turn to face her. My neck and ears are probably bright red. I glance around. All eyes are on us. Does she have to embarrass me in front of everyone?

She opens her mouth to say something, but clamps it shut. "We are not done with this discussion."

The girls are hesitant as they jump, fearing Coach's anger will turn to them, but I don't think they have anything to worry about. My gut tells me this is only about me. But is it really about me—or about my mom?

As we continue practice, the bar reaches 5'4". This is the highest I've landed to date, and my stomach feels like a hundred bees are buzzing around. I start out with long strides, counting to focus myself as my feet hit the ground. At seven steps, I start to angle toward the bar, turning sideways. Seven, eight, nine, and I drive my knee up, turning to go over the pole backwards. I land on the thick mats, bar still in place. I grin.

Only Michaela, Sasha, Katelyn, Jordyn, and I are left as Coach Clark moves the pole to 5'5." Jordyn starts her sprint to the pole. Coach Clark steps forward. "Get those knees up!"

Jordyn lifts her knee. Her foot turns, and she falls sideways. A soft gasp follows as she hits the ground and clutches her ankle. Those of us still in line circle her.

"Can you stand?" Sasha asks.

Tears well in Jordyn's eyes as she shakes her head. Coach checks Jordyn's ankle. "You're not going to be jumping anytime soon." She pulls out her phone and hands it to Jordyn. "Put in the number, and I'll talk to your parents."

We stand around while we wait for Jordyn's mom to arrive and take her to the emergency room. No one has the heart for more practice. At least none of us but Coach Clark.

"Scott!"

I spin around at Coach Clark's voice.

"You'll take Jordyn's place in high jump and long jump in county if she can't compete. You have the best chance of winning, so let's get focused on that."

High jump and long jump now? Why couldn't she have let me

do it at the beginning of season, so I'd have more practice? I clench my jaw. I can do this. I'm a freerunner. Jumping is what I do.

Practice seems endless, and I bolt from the track when it's over. Coach Clark's voice stops me. "Scott. Over here."

I hesitate. I turn to go, then stop. I've been a runner all my life, running from memories and problems. I'm going to face this one head on. I turn and walk to where Coach Clark is standing.

"Yes?"

"You're a natural at track. You said Melonie Scott is your mom, and she wasn't a runner. Okay at cheerleading but not athletic other than that. Was your dad on a track team?

"Don't know."

Her eyes bore into mine. "You don't know?"

I kick at the ground. What am I supposed to say? I don't have the answer.

She crosses her arms, and I feel her eyes on me. "What's your dad's name?"

I force myself to breathe in through my nose and release it through my mouth. I'll play it cool. I shrug one shoulder. "Don't know that either."

"Funny, because I don't remember your mom dating anyone in particular our senior year, but someone got her pregnant."

She doesn't remember my mom dating anyone? What about the guy Mom might have stolen from Coach Clark? Was that relationship with my dad? I try to sort it through in my mind, but there are too many missing pieces.

Coach Clark crosses her arms and stares at me. "She might not have been dating anyone, but I know who was working for her dad that year. I think I understand things a whole lot better now."

She might, but what does she mean about someone working for my grandfather? I shake my head and walk away. All this past drama needs to stay in the past. Coach Clark's questions were inappropriate.

Hearing a familiar engine, I turn toward the parking lot. Thorn steps out of his truck. "You coming?"

I jog to the truck. Thorn saves the day again.

"You don't have any idea why she was asking you those questions?" Thorn asks as he pulls to the curb in front of my house.

"No. And I have no clue what she meant by who worked for my grandfather either."

"You going to ask your mom?"

"If I can. Sometimes she's in the mood to talk and other times not."

I open the truck door and slide out. When I open the back door, I see my grandfather and Mom sitting at the table. They look up as I enter. My gaze goes to the object in my grandfather's hand. It's his tablet. I stare.

Mom beams. "Your grandfather is showing me pictures he's taken of all the little boys and girls at the church. He's going to have them printed out so the kids can use them to make Mother's Day cards for their moms in a few weeks. Isn't that sweet?"

My grandfather smiles, and my skin prickles. Mom is waiting for me to say something.

I nod and mutter, "Great idea," then head to my room. Did I misjudge him? Or is he fooling everyone, including Mom? Then I remember the picture of Isabella with long, dark hair cascading over her bare chest. That picture at least was not intended for a Mother's Day card.

I look back toward my grandfather. He's watching me with a smirk on his face. He knows I saw the pictures.

Chapter Fifteen

South Bay High is hosting the county meet this year. Excitement is in the air. When I arrive Friday morning at 7:30, the band members are outside in the courtyard, dressed in blue-and-gold warm-up suits similar to the game-day suits members of the track team are wearing. Music resonates throughout the grounds as the band plays the school fight song. The cement benches lining the courtyard are filled with students clapping to the music.

The fight song ends, and the students erupt into cheers. The band starts a lively number, swaying their instruments in time to the music. Wrapping their arms around each other, the students sway along with the band. The drum line hams it up for the spectators, and the quad drummer goes into a solo number. The other band members clap and stomp the beat. The spirit is contagious, and I feel a smile spreading across my face.

"Kiana, over here." I turn toward the voice. Sasha, Kendra, Michaela, and Katelyn are jamming to the music. Jordyn, supported by crutches, is there too. I jog over to join them.

"Looks like you'll have to win the 4x800 without me," Jordyn says.

I rub the back of my neck. A headache is threatening to start. "How bad is it?"

"I'm off it for at least four weeks. Besides, if I can't run county, I can't go on to district. You'll do fine without me. Coach will have Michaela or Katelyn run in my place."

I frown. "That still doesn't make it okay. I wish you were running."

Jordyn gives a half smile. "Next year. My senior year. I plan to win it all."

The band forms a circle around the edge of the courtyard, and the flag girls run into the center. Everyone backs up to give them room. The band begins playing a popular pop song, and the flag girls dance to it. They reach out and pull some of the boys from the track team into their circle.

Jordyn taps my arm. "Look." She points to a place past the parking lot. Coach Jones is running down the street toward the courtyard. He does a reverse vault over the first bike rack, mostly empty, and a dash vault over the second. He runs toward an empty cement bench in the courtyard and side vaults over it. Three front flips later Coach Jones is in the middle of the circle, dancing along with the flag girls and the boys' track team. We start clapping to the music, cheering him on. Suddenly the music stops, and the silence is met with a collective boo that echoes through the courtyard.

Coach Clark steps on the circular cement bench in the middle of the courtyard. "With all the noise, you may not have heard, but the two-minute warning bell has already rung."

She spots Coach Jones and frowns. "There will be no excused tardies, so you'd best be getting to class in a hurry." She looks toward where the girls' team is gathered. Almost every team member is present. "And that especially means you girls unless you want to run extra laps at tomorrow's practice."

I grab my backpack and sprint toward homeroom, with Kendra right beside me. "Coach can't have fun, can she? Did you see her face when she saw Coach Jones?"

"I know. Right? They're so different."

Kendra's brows knit. "Do you think Coach is nicer because of the God thing he mentioned, or is it simply a big personality difference?"

I shrug one shoulder. "Don't know. I volunteer at the Mill District City Church, helping Coach Jones with the middle-school program. He seems like the real deal. We usually have it Tuesday and Friday evenings. Someone else is leading it tonight since Coach will be at county. You should come sometime."

"I don't know if my parents would let me. They'd probably want to write a check and not have me get involved." She glances at the time on her smart phone. "We better run for it, but I have a quick stop to make."

She jogs down the hall and stops in front of Leila's locker. I stare at her. "What are you going to do?"

She grins. "Even the score." She pulls a picture and a roll of tape from her pocket. She quickly tapes the picture to Leila's locker. I lean over to see it. My eyes widen. "Is that Leila kissing Anthony—that guy who is always doing the weird stuff?"

Kendra nods.

"No way. Earlier this year he put a dissected frog on one of the cheerleader's lunch trays. He is so gross. Why in the world did Leila kiss him?"

Kendra slips a piece of paper through the locker vents. "It was at a party. The guys made a circle around a girl who was blindfolded. Someone spun her around. She had to kiss whoever was in front of her when they stopped spinning her. They pulled the blindfold off as she kissed the guy."

"Anthony was at a party with you guys?"

Red creeps up Kendra's neck. "I think he was invited just to make fun of. I can't believe I was that cruel. The note I put in her locker reminds her I also have a video of the kiss on my phone. If she doesn't want to see it on the internet, she'll back off."

I laugh. "I think that solves your problem with her."

We sprint the last few yards to homeroom and land in our chairs just as the tardy bell rings.

Chapter Sixteen

Spirits are high despite a math test. The boys' and girls' track teams are dismissed after second period to set up for the meet. I help get the hurdles ready while others set up tables for the timers and judges. We miss lunch, but Coach Jones has pizza delivered.

This is a big meet with all the county schools coming together to compete, so there are more athletes than usual. Butterflies dance in my stomach to the beat of the song the band is playing from the bleachers. The band doesn't normally play for track events, but since this is our biggest meet, they must have talked the band director into it. The music helps me stay energized for what is to come.

Thorn joins me. "Nervous?"

I rub my hands on my track shorts. "Oh, yeah. Big time."

Thorn smiles. "Don't worry about it. You've had a good track season no matter what happens today."

I try to return his smile, but it falters. "Easy for you to say. You've become a track star your first season of high school track."

"If I am, it's because I'm using what God gave me. The gift of speed, I guess."

I laugh, easing my tension. "That's almost the same thing Coach said at tryouts. God gifted us differently. Later he said he won *Running Free* because God gave him the gift of running."

Thorn grins.

I punch him playfully in the arm. "Well, whether you two are right or not, it's time to put your running to the test."

The 4x800 is announced, and the four of us take our places. Katelyn is taking Jordyn's place, leading off as the gun fires. She runs neck and neck with Holy Nativity's runner, holding first place both laps. We meet in the crossover zone, and she slaps the baton into my hand. It's a clean pass, and I'm off and running. I feel stronger than ever as I get into a steady cadence. I force myself to think of nothing but winning. I finish the first lap and hear voices cheering me on. Thorn. Katelyn. Michaela. Sasha. Coach Jones. He's standing with the others, cheering. I push myself to run even faster.

Sweat runs down my face and back as my feet fly along the ground. Kendra is waiting for me in the crossover zone. I slap the baton into her outstretched hand. Her fingers close around it as she takes off.

Coach Jones smiles as I walk over to join the others. "Good job. You've come a long way from the first practice. I expect great things out of you next year."

I grin. I hope he means it.

Our team finishes strong, first in the heat. I grab a sports drink from the cooler, then stand on the sidelines, bouncing on my toes as I watch the other events, waiting to go to the pit for high jump. Thorn runs the 1600-meter, shaving seconds off his time from last meet. Then it's time to go for high jump. Thorn walks with me. "Ready?"

I rub my hands down my track shorts. "I guess. I just hope I don't mess up and get Coach Clark angry."

"Give it your best and don't worry about it."

I stand side by side with Sasha and Michaela, waiting for the event to begin. The judges check the runway distance and the condition of the pole and bars. Then we start. The sun beats down on me as I take my place in line. Energy pulses through me as I sprint toward the pole, then curve into my J and go up and over. I land neatly on the mat and lay on my back for a couple of seconds, staring at the sky. I made it!

The pole inches up little by little. The pole is at 5'5". I take a deep breath. Can I make this? Sasha will. Me? Maybe, maybe not. The runner in front of me takes off. Turns and drives her knee up and goes over, but her heel catches the bar. She's out. I'm up.

I take another deep breath, fix my gaze on the pole, lean forward, and then start my sprint. I put all the energy I have left into the jump. I land on the mat and look up at the bar. It's still in place!

I'm not so lucky on the next jump. I clip the bar at 5'6", but I wouldn't have won anyway. Sasha takes first with a new personal record of 5'8 ½".

Long jump is immediately after high jump. Do I have anything left? I sprint down the runway, and when my feet touch the board, I launch with more strength than I thought I had. The first jump of 16'8" is my best jump of the day. My muscles feel weak, and my other jumps fall short.

Thorn is in long jump too. Like his free running, his jump is powerful and almost a work of art. He launches from the board, muscles defined. It's his best distance yet, but he only takes third place, with the first two places going to seniors. Thorn jogs back to the cooler and returns with two bottles. He thrusts a blue raspberry drink into my hand. "You need this. One more event and you'll have your first county meet behind you."

I open the bottle Thorn gave me and take a long drink. "I'm not sure I have enough energy left for the 3200-meter."

He playfully punches my arm. "You thought that before the long jump, and you did great."

I take a sip of the drink, the coolness refreshing me. "Only fifth place. And that's only because of freerunning. Maybe next year Coach Clark will let me do high jump and long jump as my regular events."

Thorn nods. "I think she will. Sasha is graduating, and you're the second-best jumper. I don't know why she didn't let you jump this year, but she'd be foolish to keep you from it again next year. Besides, after doing so well in county, Coach Jones would probably make her allow you to do high jump."

I nod and focus on the meet. The excitement in the air carries me through the 3200-meter, but I only place fourth. I'm not one of the three going to district for this event. Next year. I laugh. When did I become so sure about next year?

When all the events have finished, the judges go over the scores one more time. Then the award ceremony starts. My spirits swell as I accept my ribbon for the 4x800. First in county. Not bad for my first year, but I know it was Sasha and Michaela who carried us.

Many of the runners from both the boys' and girls' teams are going on to district as well as some from the field events. The season is over for the track team members who didn't place in the top three for any of their events. I feel bad for those athletes, but I'm excited for those of us who are going on.

Chapter Seventeen

Practices are grueling the next week, so I'm relieved when it's finally Friday again. Thorn has to work, so I jog the three miles to the church. When I arrive and go inside, I notice the younger kids who haven't been picked up yet are heading out to the fenced-in playground.

Coach comes through the door with a few of the freerunners from the group. He smiles. "It's beautiful out. Let's go to the playground out back and play a follow-the-leader game with the moves we've taught them. You up for it?"

"Sure. But some of the after-school kids are out there playing while they wait for pick-up."

"We'll stay near the back on the bigger equipment."

Coach leads us out a back door onto the playground. It's not bad. Smaller than the school playground, but it has a sturdy swing set, bars you cross hand over hand, and even a couple of low, square structures made of bars that resemble cages. There is a low balance beam and a yellow plastic tunnel, plus two child-sized benches and a small shed. Some of the children are taking big wheel trike from the shed, while others play in a different section that has several plastic climbing sets.

There's a lot of potential here. I turn to Coach. "What do you have in mind?"

Coach looks around. "Why don't you lead off, and I'll follow you? Then the others can follow us."

I jog toward the cubes, jump, grasping the bars with my arms shoulder-width apart, then swing my legs through and land on the ground. Coach follows me with Chance, Robert, and Drake right behind him. I see Isabella and Malakai playing with a group of children on a plastic climbing set. Isabella looks up and waves. I wave back.

Parents are coming to the gate. Carolyn hands them the clipboard to sign, then they leave with their child. Only a few children are left. Isabella is one of them.

We continue around the playground, swinging hand over hand on the bars and crawling over the tunnel. I look over to see if Isabella is watching, but Carolyn is taking three kids, including Isabella, back into the church.

My grandfather approaches Carolyn. He says something to her, then walks over, closes and padlocks the gate. Without looking our way, he walks back into the church. Why is he still here? It's past time for the younger kids to leave. Why aren't their parents here yet?

Chance jumps in front of me. "What are we waiting for? Let's go. Or are you out of moves?"

I shake my head and try to focus on our freerunning follow-the-leader game. It's no use. My stomach is knotting. Something is not right. The picture of Isabella on the iPad floods my mind. I turn to Coach. "I need to go in for a minute."

His brows furrow. "Are you okay?"

"Just my stomach," I say. It's true enough.

Coach looks at Chance. "This is your turn to lead. You go ahead, and the others will follow you."

Chance beams. "All right. Now you're talking."

I slip into the church as quietly as possible so my grandfather and Carolyn won't notice me. Carolyn is talking to a young man, who then takes the hand of a young boy and leaves the gym. I look around. There's only one child left and no sign of my grandfather or Isabella. My breathing quickens. There wasn't time for Isabella to leave yet. Besides, I would have seen her leaving. My gut tells me she's with my grandfather, but where are they?

I glance around one more time before heading down the hall to the restrooms. Apprehension creeps up my spine as I walk down the corridor. I crack open the girls' restroom door. Nothing. I push the boys' door open. Empty. Where is he? The hall ends at a set of metal doors.

Pushing the doors open, I see my grandfather and Isabella. He has her by the hand, heading to his car. I race after him. "Hey!

Hey, stop!"

He turns. A flicker of anger brushes across his face before he smiles. "What seems to be the problem, Kiana?" Before I can answer, he looks down at Isabella. "This is my granddaughter. Do you know her?"

Isabella nods. "From the bathroom, remember?"

I interrupt. "What are you doing? Where are you going?"

Isabella smiles at me. "He's taking me home cause sometimes my mom forgets to come and get me."

I stare at my grandfather. "You can't do that. If you were allowed, you wouldn't be sneaking out the back door."

He smiles again and pulls Isabella to him. "Of course, I can. And I'm going out the back door because it's closer to where I'm parked."

"Let's go ask Carolyn about that." I reach for Isabella, but she grips my grandfather's hand.

I squat down so I'm eye to eye with her. "Your mom would never forget you. She's just late tonight. Let's go up and wait with Carolyn."

I look over her head at my grandfather, and my breath catches. His smile is still in place, but his eyes are pure ice.

"We need to go in," I tell Isabella, taking her hand. She reluctantly follows me.

Carolyn is heading our way, looking worried. "Oh, there you are. Isabella's mother is here looking for her. What are you doing out here?"

"My grandfather was getting ready to take her home," I say. I doubt that's true, but I'm repeating his story, hoping Carolyn will do something about it.

Her lips tighten. "Surely you misunderstood your grandfather," she says, looking at me. "No one can take a child from the premises without the written consent of the parent."

My grandfather opens his mouth, but before he can say anything, Isabella speaks. "He was going to take me home because my mom forgot me. He was helping me."

Carolyn looks from Isabella to my grandfather. My grandfather smiles his most charming smile. "I was just telling her that if her mom ever needed help getting her home, I could do that."

Carolyn frowns. "That would be inappropriate. An adult volunteer should never be alone with any child." She reaches for Isabella's hand. "Let's go. Your mom is waiting."

I clench my teeth. He's lying to her. Can't she see that? He hasn't changed, but how do I convince anyone?

My grandfather turns to me, almost as though he has read my thoughts. But before he can say anything, the freerun group enters the gym, followed by Coach Jones.

My grandfather studies him, and a look of pure hatred crosses his face, but almost as soon as it's there, it's gone. He turns to me. "That's your track coach, isn't it?"

"You would only know that if you were spying on me at track," I say.

My grandfather's eyes narrow, but then he smiles. "Since when is watching my granddaughter practice or at a meet considered spying?"

I study my grandfather's face, but it gives nothing away. He's up to something, but I can't imagine what that would be. Still, I'm sure it's not good.

My grandfather watches Coach for another minute, then turns and walks out the door without another word.

Chapter Eighteen

I don't want to go home. I don't know why my grandfather was at my practices or why he looked at Coach Jones with such hatred. Maybe my imagination is working overtime, but I do have a good idea about why he was taking Isabella out the back door and to his car.

I take my time getting home, but I have to face my grandfather sooner or later. When I enter the house, he and Mom are at the table drinking coffee. My grandfather looks up at me, then turns his gaze to Mom. "Has Kiana told you about her track coach? The same man she's working with at the church?"

Mom glances at her dad and then at me. "I thought Cassandra Clark was your track coach?"

"She's the assistant coach who works with the girls," I say.

My grandfather smiles, a smile that doesn't reach his eyes and makes me want to gag. He looks at Mom. "Her head coach is Terrence Jones."

Mom lets go of the mug she's holding. It hits the table and drops onto the floor, spewing coffee everywhere. I rush to the kitchen drawer, pull out a handful of dish towels, run back to the table, and catch the liquid spilling onto the floor. I wipe the spilled coffee from the floor, taking my time while my mind tries to process what just happened. Why did Coach Jones name trigger that response?

I look at Mom. She's staring at my grandfather, mouth open. "Terrence Jones? He's back?"

My grandfather nods. "Coaching at the high school and volunteering at the church. And your daughter is working side-by-side with him."

Mom looks toward me. Her mouth opens as though she's going to say something, but then she snaps it closed.

"What ..." I don't know how to finish my question.

"You ... you stay away from that man." Mom's tone is harsh. Her voice catches. "That man is no good. Nothing but a thief."

Now my mouth drops open. "A thief? No. He talks to the kids about God. He's a good guy. You're thinking of someone else."

My grandfather smirks. My breath catches. What's his game?

"No, Kiana. She's thinking of the right guy. He used to work for me at my car dealership. He wanted to go to college, and I gave him a job to help him out. What did he do to thank me? Stole from me. That's what he did. Took my money. Hid it in his car."

I turn to Mom. "That's not true. It can't be. He's not that kind of person. He's amazing with the kids."

"You might think he's a good guy, but I know what he really is," Mom says.

My grandfather smiles. "I think it's a good idea if you don't go to the church again. We don't want to see you get hurt."

I stare at him. "You don't want to see me get hurt? You're the only one who has ever hurt me. And you can't tell me what to do. You're not my mother."

My mother frowns. "Your grandfather is right. You shouldn't go back to the church. Terrence Jones is not someone you need to be hanging out with."

Heat rushes through me. "No, your dad is the one who shouldn't go back. Ask him about Isabella. How he had her shirt off in the restroom. How he tried to take her from the church."

Confusion crosses Mom's face, and she turns toward her father. "What's that about?"

"It was nothing. Nothing at all. Just a misunderstanding, and now Kiana is using it to take the attention from herself." He turns to me. "We were talking about you and why you shouldn't go back to the church. I'm merely volunteering with the after-school program and attending the senior citizens' activities. Your mother already knows that."

I glare at my grandfather, then spin on my heel and go to my room. I shut the door and lay on my bed, willing myself to relax. Minutes pass, and there's a knock at the door. I ignore it, and the door opens part way.

Mom comes in and sits on the edge of my bed. "You might think Terrence is a nice guy, but he's not. He was in my class. We worked together at Dad's auto shop. He was a thief."

"You really believe he stole from your father?"

"He told me he did it. And the money was found in his car." Mom wraps her arms around herself. "I don't want to talk about it. Just take my word for it. I trusted him, and he shattered my trust. Stay away from him."

"I can't. He's the head track coach. And Cassandra Clark is the girl's coach. What's this all about? Does it have to do with Coach Clark? She can't stand him." My voice is shaky. I try to control it, but I can't. "I need more answers than that he's a thief and stole from your father. Who, by the way, has been stalking me at track practice."

"Kiana! Stalking you? Where do you come up with this? What's wrong with him wanting to watch you?"

"Hiding in bushes and behind trees instead of sitting in the stands with other spectators? And when he does sit in the stands, it's with girls my age." A thought hits me and spills out my mouth. "Or was he stalking Coach Jones? Waiting to stir up trouble for him?"

Mom gets up and walks to the door. She looks back at me. "I can't talk about this anymore. Just take my word for it. He's not what he appears."

"Is he the one?" I call after her. "The guy you stole from Cassandra Clark? Was that him?"

There's nothing but the sound of Mom's retreating steps. I flip my phone open to call Thorn. I fill him in, then lean back on my bed, trying to process it all. Did Mom like Coach Jones? I can't picture that. Still, she was a cheerleader, and he was a track star.

My brain races. Coach Clark said something about knowing who worked for my grandfather. Did she mean Coach Jones? Does she know he stole from my grandfather, and that's why she doesn't like him? It's because of theft, not a broken heart? I close my eyes. I can't think about this anymore. It's draining me.

I startle awake and sit up. I must have fallen asleep for a few minutes. What is that pounding noise? It's coming from my window. I pull the curtain aside and stifle a shriek. Thorn is peering in. He laughs as I open the window.

"You scared me to death."

He grins. "Not literally. You're still alive."

"What are you doing here?"

"I thought a run on the beach would help."

"After dark? On a Friday night?"

"Sure. Why not?"

I lock my door and follow him out my window, leaving it cracked so I can get back in. We climb into Thorn's truck, and he pulls onto Highway 98 West toward the beach.

I lean my head back against the seat and close my eyes. Next thing I know, Thorn is shaking me awake. I climb out of the truck and walk to the sand.

"Barefoot," Thorn says.

"Barefoot?"

Thorn nods and pulls off his shoes. I pull off my shoes and socks and tuck the socks into the shoes. I step onto the sand and shiver. It's cool with the sundown.

"You'll warm up," Thorn says. "Let's stretch out."

We stretch, then start down the beach at a jog. It feels different running on sand. I breathe in through my nose and out my mouth.

Thorn runs in silence beside me. I know he'll wait for me to talk or let me run in silence.

"I can't believe what my grandfather said about Coach Jones—that he's a thief. It doesn't fit anything we know about him."

"Did you ask your mom about it?"

I stop jogging and stand facing the dark water. "She told me he was no good and a thief and I should stay away from him. He broke her trust."

"There has to be an explanation," Thorn says. "I'd trust Coach Jones over your grandfather. Besides, the school would have run a background check before hiring him. If he had a record, he wouldn't be our coach."

"That's true. It would be one thing if my grandfather said it, but Mom backed him up. What am I supposed to believe? Coach talks about believing in God and stuff, but what if Coach Jones isn't who we think he is?"

I start to shiver, and Thorn pulls me against him for warmth. I lay my head against his chest. Stars twinkle over our heads.

Thorn sighs. "I wish I had easy answers. All I know is that believing there is a God who cares makes the hard stuff easier for me to handle. I have a peace about it. Most of it, at least. Still working on the thing with my dad. I'd rather believe someone has a plan than that all of this stuff is random and nothing good will come of it."

I stare into the night sky. Maybe Thorn is right, and maybe he's not. Too many thoughts compete for my attention.

Thorn drives me home. I pull myself up the rail and cross the porch roof to my room. My window is closed and so are my shades. I know I left the shades open and window cracked when I left. I grab the window frame and try to pull up, but it won't budge. The shades slowly open. I look up and stifle a scream. My grandfather is standing in the window looking out at me. I take a step back. My foot lands on one of the rotted spots, and it gives way. My foot plunges through and I have to move to a firm spot quickly to avoid the whole roof giving way and dumping me on the porch below.

My grandfather raises the shades and opens the window but remains standing in front of it. He chuckles, but there's nothing friendly about it. "I'm sure your mother would find it very interesting you sneak in and out of your window."

I jam my hands in my pockets to keep them from shaking as I feign indifference. "My mother wouldn't care."

"Then by all means, come on in." He steps aside, but I don't trust him. I cautiously move forward and put one leg through the window, duck my head, and slip into my room. When I straighten up, I'm left facing my grandfather.

My grandfather's smile is replaced by something harder. Something almost evil. "Your mom may not care what is going on with you, but I do. You think Terrence Jones is someone special, but he's not. What's more, I ran him off once before, and I can do it again. I still have evidence proving that he stole from me."

"What evidence?"

"None of your business. Just stay out of my way, or Coach Jones is going to find his life a lot harder. Where would your team be without a head coach? Do you want to find out? Because I can make that happen."

Chapter Nineteen

"Get out of my room," I say through clenched teeth. "Now."

He starts to say something but stops as footsteps sound on the steps. Mom appears in my doorway. "What is going on up here? Why are you up so late, Kiana?"

My grandfather smiles. "No worries. We were simply talking about the church program. Kiana understands about staying away from Coach Jones and the church." He brushes past Mom, enters his room, and closes the door.

Mom turns to me, "Are you okay with it? Not going to the church, I mean?"

I drop to my bed and pull my knees to my chest. "No, I'm not okay with it. I'm helping with the freerunning group. Coach Jones really cares about them. He gives up his Tuesday and Friday evenings to be with them. That doesn't sound like something a criminal would do. How can you be sure he stole money?"

"He told me, Kiana. I asked him, and he told me he took the money. He wouldn't tell me why. Do you know how that made me feel? I thought he liked me, and instead he was just using me."

I walk to my window and look outside, then I turn back to face Mom. "You liked him? As in boy-girl liked him?"

"It was a long time ago. That's not important now. What's important is that he wasn't who I thought he was. He stole from my dad. The money was in his car. He confessed to it."

I shake my head. "You can believe that, but I don't. He's a good role model to the kids. But your dad? He's targeting a little girl named Isabella. She's six, and she looks a lot like I did at that age."

Mom sighs. "What makes you think he's targeting her? He said he's like a grandfather to the younger kids because a lot of them don't have a male role model in their homes."

"He had Isabella in the men's bathroom washing out her shirt.

And he was trying to take her to his car. He said he was taking her home."

Mom is silent.

"He wasn't supposed to be doing either of those things. A man can't take a little girl into the men's restroom and take her shirt off. And he can't take a child from the church no matter the reason."

Mom sighs. "Kiana, he is just trying to do some good with his life. Can't you be happy about that? He's attending the senior citizen group at church and their Wednesday morning Bible study."

"Bible study? What is that? They sit there and read the Bible? Why can't he do that at home? Why go to the church where there are little girls—and Coach Jones?"

"They read the Scriptures. They have a book that explains what it means. Your grandfather showed me. He had even written in the answers to the questions about the Scriptures they are studying. Doesn't that show you he's changed?"

"He has a book that has questions in it about the Bible? Like a schoolbook?"

"It's smaller, and it's written for men's Bible study groups."

I shake my head. Bible study groups? The word Bible doesn't even belong in the same sentence as my Grandfather's name. And now Mom is more convinced than ever that he's changed. And I'm more convinced than ever that he's a clever actor.

I wake up Saturday morning and jump out of bed. Then I remember there's no meet today. Next Saturday is the district meet hosted by Central. I jog to Thorn's and knock on the door. He lets me in. Good smells greet me. "It smells happy in here," I say.

Thorn's grandfather nods. "I agree. Nothing like the smell of pancakes, bacon, and grits. Come join us. We were just getting ready to eat."

We gather around the table, and Thorn's grandfather says a prayer before we eat. Then he turns to me. "I hear you're going to the district track meet."

"Yes. And thank you again for the shoes. I couldn't have done it without them."

He smiles at me, and his eyes crinkle. "Glad I could help. Especially if they helped you qualify for districts."

Talk turns to track until we're done eating. Then Thorn and I clear the table and start washing dishes. I tell him about my grandfather waiting at my window.

He frowns. "That's creepy."

I nod. "Not only that, but he said he still has evidence proving that Coach Jones stole from him. That he ran him off once before and he can do it again. It's like he's threatening me to stay out of his business, or he'll take it out on Coach Jones."

Thorn washes a plate and puts it in the dish rack. "And your mom backed him up?"

"Not on that part. She wasn't in my room yet. But when she came in, she said she'd liked Coach Jones—like boyfriend kind of liked—and that he just used her."

"You think they dated?"

"Not with my grandfather. He'd never let her date an African American. Although she did sort of say she stole a guy from Coach Clark. You think that was him?"

"Ask her."

"I did, and she ignored me. I think there's more to it."

Thorn turns and looks at me.

"What? Why are you staring at me?"

"Your grandfather would never let her date an African American, yet you are part African American."

I stare at him. "What are you saying?"

"What if he's your dad?"

My mouth drops open. "Coach Jones? No way."

Thorn silently studies me.

"What?"

"The shape of your face is similar to his. The shape of your eyes."

"He's a lot darker than I am. I think my mom was with someone lighter or even part white."

Thorn shakes his head. "She wouldn't have to. There was a show on television last month where an African American couple had a child who was almost white because there was someone back a couple of generations who was white. And there was also a white woman and black man on the show. They gave birth to twins. One was white, the other black."

"Coach told us he left here the day after graduation. My mom said she got pregnant after graduation, but that I came early, so it makes it look like she was pregnant before graduation. Coach would have been gone by time she got pregnant."

Thorn lets the subject drop, but I can tell he thinks he's right. I change the subject. "I'm more concerned about my grandfather anyway. There's just too much about him that bothers me."

"Like?"

"Like, does he really have cancer? Is that really why he's here? Why move to the poor section if you have a fancy house somewhere else? For that matter, why did he move from his house in the first place, and where did he move to?"

Thorn chuckles. "That's a lot of questions. You could try doing a search on him using one of the computers in the school library. You could do it before school."

"I'm not sure where I'd start."

"I'll help you. I'll pick you up early on Monday. If you need answers, we'll find answers."

Chapter Twenty

A thousand butterflies fill my stomach Monday morning as we drive to school. Thorn seems confident and upbeat. He glances sideways at me. "I used the tablet my grandfather has for work and went to a bounty hunter website for ideas on how to find out about people."

"We know where my grandfather is. We're not trying to find him."

"Right. But there are some places to look for past addresses and stuff. I'll show you when we get on the computer."

We arrive at school early. The lot is almost empty. When we reach the library, Thorn signs the clipboard for a computer, and we go to the one we're assigned. It's already up and ready to be used. Thorn types in a web address, and a site opens. He turns to me. "The more information we have about your grandfather, the more it'll tell us. Full name?"

"Walter Edmund Scott. Mom said he was named for both his grandfathers."

Thorn types in the name. "Do you know his birthday or social security number?"

"His birthday. Only because it's next week and Mom wants to do something to celebrate. It's April 4. He'll be 64." I pull out a composition book I brought along to write down anything we find out.

Thorn types in the date and hits enter. We wait as the computer searches, then displays the information. Thorn studies it. "Hmm. That's funny."

"What?"

"Well, it lists four different addresses since the one where your mom grew up. Looks like he moved not long after you and your mom left."

"Four in the past eight years? How would he be able to run a business if he moved so often? Was it all within the same city?"

Thorn shakes his head. "No. The first place was Montgomery, Alabama. It lists his place of work as Scott Motors, so he owned his own company again. Then he moved to Biloxi, Mississippi. Then Shreveport, Louisiana. The last place was Valdosta, Georgia. Alabama is the only one that lists a place of work."

I jot down the cities in my notebook. "So, he didn't work in the other cities?"

"I don't know if he didn't work or they didn't list it. He lived in Montgomery for almost four of the eight years, and then he moved almost every year. Wonder why?"

"Apartments or house? How would he buy and sell houses that quickly?"

Thorn clicks on the first address and cuts it. He opens a location site, enters the address and hits find. It pulls up a small white house with hedges along the front of the house and a large tree in the front yard. "Looks nice ... kind of house I'd like some day."

"Me too," I agree.

Thorn cuts and pastes the address in Biloxi. It brings up a duplex. "This was probably a rental," Thorn says.

"Not bad though. I'd live there."

"Me too," Thorn agrees as he cuts and pastes the next address. An apartment building pops up. "Huh. The address doesn't list an apartment number."

I look at the picture. "Maybe it's a mistake?"

"Doubt it. This site is pretty accurate."

Thorn cut and pastes the last address. "Address not found" pops up on the screen. Before I can say anything, the warning bell rings.

"We'll have to finish this later," Thorn says. "Before school tomorrow."

I try to concentrate during school, but my mind keeps going back to how many times my grandfather moved. Four addresses. Four different states. And the only employment listed was his own company. Why move so often, and how would you maintain a business with so many moves?

I head to track practice after school. It looks empty with only those of us going on to district next Friday and Saturday at practice. Coach calls all of us, boys and girls, to the bleachers. "We have a lot to do in the next four practices. We'll be working together in order to get the most done. I'll work with the relays, running, and hurdles here at the track. Coach Clark will take those doing field events. If you are in both, you'll start here with me, and then go over to her once we've practiced your event. Let's have 100-meter on the track first."

Coach Clark leads her group to the field events area while the sprinters take their places on the track. Practice goes quickly with both coaches pushing us hard to be ready for the weekend meet.

After practice, Thorn and I walk back to his truck. Coach Jones grins his lopsided grin as we pass him. "See you both tomorrow night?"

I pause. I feel Thorn looking at me. I shake my head. Coach's smile fades to a confused look. "No? Too much homework?"

I look at the ground and kick a pebble, sending it flying.

"Kiana?"

I look up and into his eyes. Does Mom really believe he is a thief? These aren't the eyes of a thief.

"Is something wrong?" he asks.

I kick at another pebble. "No, I ... I just can't go to the church right now."

An awkward silence hangs in the air.

"You'd tell me if something was wrong?"

I shrug. "I have to go." I turn away and head for Thorn's truck. I don't need to see Coach Jones to know he's watching me.

When I get home, Mom is already there. "Got off early," she says. She pours herself a cup of coffee and sits at the table. She wraps her hands around the mug. I sit across from her.

"Is your dad at the church?" I don't want to ask her about him and then find out he's listening in.

"I think so."

"You said we moved out of your dad's house after your mom died, right?"

She nods. "Yes, we moved to this house."

"What did your dad do? I mean in the years between when we left and when he showed up here in February?"

Mom gives me a puzzled look. "Why do you want to know?"

"I was just wondering. I know he moved out of town sometime after Grandma died."

"He moved to Alabama. He had a chance to buy a car lot there from a friend who was retiring."

"And then?"

"What do you mean by and then?"

"He lived more places after that. Why did he leave Alabama?"

Mom gives me another puzzled look. "Who told you that? He never left Alabama. He's lived there ever since he left here."

My mind spins. Should I tell her what Thorn and I found out? I decided to wait until we learn more. I get orange juice from the fridge and pour some in a glass before changing the subject. "He doesn't really seem sick. Has he gone to the doctor since he's been here?"

Mom nods. "I went with him once."

"Did you talk to the doctor?"

"No, why would I?"

"Just wondered. It seems like he'd be getting worse by now if he had cancer."

Mom's brows lower. "He has cancer. That much I know. It's inoperable. What's with all the questions today?"

I sip my juice. I know she won't like what I'm going to say. "I don't trust him. I told you about the little girl ... Isabella. I don't like the way he's acting toward her. What if he does something to her?"

Mom rubs her thumb up and down the handle of her mug. "He won't. He enjoys going to the church and helping out with the children. He said he's like a grandfather to them."

"He is my grandfather, and you know what he did to me."

"That was a long time ago."

"If you're wrong, another little girl may get hurt."

"Didn't you say that lady—Carolyn—has a lot of rules in place? I'm sure nothing will go wrong." Mom stands and puts her cup in the sink, signaling the end of the discussion.

Thorn and I go back to the library the next morning. He brings up the same site, and we get the same "address not found" message. "What next?" I ask.

"We find sites specific to Montgomery, like newspaper archives and public records, to see what turns up."

He taps some keys, and we're in another site. He types in my grandfather's name. Pictures of my grandfather with a T-ball team fill the screen. Acid creeps into my throat. All little girls. Several of them with light-brown skin, brown eyes, and dark-brown hair like my own. "Oh no. This is not good. I can't believe he merely sponsored this team. I bet he targeted at least one of them. Could that be why he moved to four different states?"

"Possibly," Thorn says. "We can check if he's a registered sex offender, but the church probably screened him already."

"But if he moved out of state, would a background check catch it?"

"If he's a registered sex offender, maybe. Otherwise, probably not," Thorn says. "That could be why he kept moving." He taps some keys and brings up a new website. He types in my grandfather's name, but nothing comes up.

"My mom didn't even know he moved. She thinks he lived in Montgomery the whole eight years."

"Did you tell her?"

"No, I wanted to wait to see what we find out."

Thorn glances at the computer. "Not enough. We know that he moved, but we don't know why."

"How else would we get information? Like what if he did something to one of the girls but it couldn't be proved?"

Thorn's brows scrunch together. "Maybe a mother would chat about it. Or post to a social media site. Maybe post in a blog."

Thorn types "Walter Scott" into the search engine and clicks on "blogs." Random links come up. I suggest, "Try putting 'Walter Scott' in parenthesis so you only get links if it's an exact match."

Thorn does that, and a shorter list of links comes up. Some are obviously not what we're looking for. There's a city-sponsored blog that features his car lot. It also has another picture of my grandfather posing with a girls' team, holding a trophy. Thorn scrolls down until he comes to a blog titled "Amber's Mom." When he clicks the link, it opens to an entry from five years ago. The name Walter Scott is in bold since that was the search term. Thorn skims the blog entry. His eyes widen. "I think we found it."

"What does it say?"

Thorn turns to me. "It's from Montgomery. It said that Scott Motors was the sponsor of this Amber's T-ball team. I guess that means your grandfather paid for their uniforms or something. He attended all their team games. One day, a mom saw him putting one of the players, I guess the Amber whose mom is writing this blog, in his car. When she asked him what he was doing, he said he was taking the little girl home because her mom hadn't shown up for the game. The other mom told Amber's mom, who had to work late but was on her way. She had not given your grandfather permission to drive her daughter home. She tried to report it, but he insisted he was just trying to help. Amber's mom took her off the team."

"That sounds just like what he tried with Isabella. I wonder how many other times he's tried that."

Thorn shrugs. "I don't know. Let's keep looking."

We click on a few of the links that look promising, but there's nothing there other than mentions of him donating to one children's group or another.

Thorn sucks in a breath.

"What?"

"This might explain why he left Montgomery. It's from the local crime and courts news section of the Montgomery newspaper four years ago. Listen. 'Local businessman Walter Scott was arrested yesterday on the accusation of attempting to remove a five-year-old girl from a Montgomery City Park after-school program under the guise of taking her home. He pled not guilty and was released on a fifty-thousand-dollar bond.'"

"Wow. I wonder what happened in the investigation?"

Thorn shakes his head. "There's nothing else. And it's dated just a few weeks before he left Montgomery, according to what we found yesterday."

I snorted. "As usual, he probably managed to talk himself out of the charges, especially if the girls were like Isabella and think he's their best friend. Guess it spooked him enough to leave and start over somewhere else."

The warning bell rings, and Thorn shuts down the computer. He turns to me. "Looks like he's got quite a habit of offering little girls car rides under the pretense of taking them home. He seems to target park and recreation leagues that are for low-income kids, the ones more likely to have single parents who have to work and might not get off in time to pick up their kids."

I clench my fist. "So he takes advantage of that to lure the little ones into going somewhere with him. He probably offers them ice cream or something to get them to go with him, shows them a little attention, and then ... does what he does. They might not even tell anyone because of the attention and treats."

Thorn frowns. "That's sick, but I'm sure you're right."

"It's how my grandfather works." I stop. I don't want to think back, but my mind goes there anyway—to the day I was spinning round and round in my pink dress, thinking I was a princess. First my grandfather took me out for ice cream, and then ...

I shake my head. Not going there.

By the time we log off the computer, I barely make it to class before the tardy bell rings. Announcements are being read, but my mind is still trying to process what we've learned. Someone writes a blog post about my grandfather trying to take a girl from a baseball field. Then he actually gets arrested for the same thing. He may have managed to wiggle his way out of that accusation, but something spooked him enough to make him leave Montgomery.

Was he afraid that the public disclosure of an investigation might result in more parents showing up to accuse him? Maybe someone whose little girl he'd already hurt and gotten away with it? Or who might not have known what he'd done at the time, but added it up when they read the news report?

More urgently now, I wondered if what we found would be

enough to get my mom to listen to my concerns? Or for the lady from the church to believe me over my grandfather? Or would it take something more to get people to see my grandfather for what he is?

Chapter Twenty-One

Thoughts about what we learned are never far from my mind, but track is also getting more intense. On Tuesday, we have a short practice since Coach doesn't want to wear us out before Friday. After track practice, Thorn drives me home. He pulls up in front of my house. Mom isn't home yet, and I assume my grandfather is at the after-school program at the church.

Thorn turns to me. "So, you aren't going tonight?"

"Mom doesn't want me around Coach Jones at all. I don't want to push it with district meet coming up."

Thorn nods, but his face reflects disapproval.

"What? There's nothing I can do about it. This is my grandfather's doing."

"Maybe in more ways than one," Thorn says.

"What do you mean?"

"I have trouble believing Coach stole money from your grandfather."

"Me too, but it was found in his car. Maybe he really was a different person back then."

Thorn's eyes narrow. "Do you really believe that? For one thing, he's too smart to leave stolen money in his car."

"Maybe, but it would have been the word of a high school boy against a well-known businessman. Just like right now. If I try to warn anyone about my grandfather, it'll look like I'm a poor sport because I can't work with the church program anymore."

I try to focus on my homework, but my mind keeps going to the church program. I slam my book shut. I may as well clean the house. No one has done it lately, and maybe it'll take my mind away from the kids who are leaving the after-school program about now.

I grab the vacuum cleaner from the closet. The duct tape patching the hose is starting to pull off. I find a roll of tape and wrap the new adhesive around the old, then start vacuuming the carpets. My mind is whirling as I push the machine, making patterns on the carpet. Is Isabella at the church right now? Is my grandfather there too? I yank on the vacuum cleaner and drag it across the floor. I realize the bag needs to be changed. When I pull off the cover and detach the bag, dust spills onto the floor. Great! Now I have to vacuum that area all over again. I dump the bag in the kitchen trash. Why can't I rid my life of all the junk as easily? I put the machine back together and resume my job, trying to force my thoughts to the upcoming district meet. When I finish vacuuming, my spirit remains unsettled. I may as well vacuum upstairs, since I can't focus on anything anyway. There isn't any carpeting, but the bedroom rugs need cleaning. I flip on the light in the room Mom is using, then start pushing the vacuum across the rug. The whole floor is a mess. I change the machine setting for bare floors and vacuum the rest. Next, I do the same for my room.

I hesitate outside my grandfather's room. I don't really want to vacuum, but this would be a good chance to snoop, though I know he's too smart to leave anything lying around. I flip on the light. If he comes home, he'll hear the vacuum cleaner and know why I'm in his room.

I vacuum between his bed and the wall. Nothing new on the nightstand, just more books. As I push the vacuum cleaner forward, I hit the nightstand leg and send his pile of books to the floor. Pictures have fallen from the books. As I reach to scoop up the books, I wonder whether they were in a book or merely between the books. I lean over to scoop up the pictures. The first is a shot of a house. The numbers 1530 are on the front, but I don't know what street. The next looks like it was taken through the window of a little girl's room.

My heart starts to race. It's Isabella's room. I can see her in the room, wearing a cute pair of pink pajamas. The next photo is a close-up of Isabella. I can make out the kitten picture on her pajama top. The last picture shows Isabella's mother sitting on her bed, tucking her in. The pictures are innocent enough, but taking them through a window is not. Why did he have these printed? Why not keep them on his tablet where they wouldn't be seen?

I pick up two pieces of paper that also had fallen from one of the books. The smaller piece of paper is a receipt from a pizza place known for its video arcade. My grandfather went there? According to the receipt, he bought two regular drinks, a princess cup, a large pizza, and fifty tokens. Heat rushes through me. For a moment I have trouble focusing on what I'm seeing. Then the questions come. Did he take Isabella and her mother to the pizza place? He sure didn't take me or Mom. Is he trying to win Isabella's mom's trust? If he wins her trust, getting to Isabella won't be a problem at all. She'll readily go with him for a treat, like he did to me with the ice cream.

The second piece of paper is folded into thirds. As I unfold it, my heart plummets. It's a permission form signed by Isabella's mom, allowing my grandfather to take Isabella home if needed. I resist the urge to rip it to shreds but instead, I refold it, and set it with the pile of books on the nightstand.

What do I do? I know my first call will be to Thorn, but then what? Who do I talk to? Carolyn will tell me how wonderful it is that my grandfather is willing to help a single mother. Mom will try to convince me that he's just trying to be a father figure to Isabella. Would Coach listen? But I'm not supposed to talk to him. Still, if I tell him who my grandfather is, that might make a difference. If he used to work for my grandfather, he probably already knows what kind of man he is. But what about the evidence that proves Coach stole from him? Is there any truth to that?

I carry the vacuum cleaner downstairs. Glancing at the clock, I note that my grandfather should be home by now. Where is he? I can't shake the feeling that everything is not okay. I flip open my phone and call Thorn.

"What's up?"

His voice calms me, and I tell him what I found.

"What are you going to do?"

"I'm not supposed to go to the church, but I'm going."

"To do what?"

I look at the time on my phone. "The after-school kids would have left already, but I have a bad feeling. I want to check on Isabella. She probably left the church long ago, but what if my grandfather took her? Remember the incidents we found online? That's how he works. He acts like the good guy, taking the girls home. But I don't even know where she lives, just that the house number is 1530."

"It should have been on the form giving your grandfather permission to take her home," Thorn says.

"You're right. I'm going to check."

I run up to my grandfather's room and pull the paper out. Sure enough, the note, written in small letters, gives him permission to take Isabella to 1530 South Sixth. I tell Thorn the address. "I've got to go to the church to make sure she was picked up by her mom. I need to know she's okay. If not, I'll find this address and make sure she's okay."

"I'll come get you. I'm walking out the door now."

Minutes later, I hear Thorn's truck approaching. When he pulls up to the curb, I quickly climb in. As Thorn drives, I reach into my pocket, grasp my Statue of Liberty coin, and squeeze.

Thorn slows down as we reach the church. The playground is empty, and my grandfather's car is nowhere to be seen.

"What now?" he asks.

"Drive by her house?"

Thorn turns to me. "And do what?"

I shrug. "I don't know. See if everything looks okay?"

Thorn drives past the church and continues to South Sixth. He turns left onto the street. "Do you see the numbers?"

"This one is 1422." I look ahead. "The next one is 1426. We're going the right way."

Thorn continues down the road. We reach the next block and find 1530. It's a small one-story house bordered by a narrow alley. "No sign of your grandfather."

"Pull down the alley. Maybe he's parked in back."

Thorn pulls slowly into the alley, trying to avoid potholes, his truck brushing against shrubs on both sides. A few yards down the alley, I spot my grandfather's silver convertible in the backyard of Isabella's house. Part of me knew it would be there even though I'd hoped it wouldn't be. The car is almost hidden behind bushes. A run-down chain-link fence surrounds the backyard, an opening where a gate should be. "There it is."

Thorn pulls up behind the car. "What do you want to do?"

Heat rushes through me, and the visions start. Me in my pink dress. The ice cream. Going into my grandfather's room when we got home to play the game he'd promised. I squeeze my eyes shut and force the pictures out. I picture Isabella in her kitty pajamas and know what we have to do. "If he's hurting her, we have to stop him."

Thorn grips the steering wheel. "But what if we burst in there and he's calmly sitting at the table eating supper with Isabella and her mom?"

I sigh. "Then he comes off as the good grandfather, and I'm the bad one. But if he's not up to something, why not just park in front? Why scratch up his car by parking in the bushes?"

I already know the answer. It's time for us to act.

Chapter Twenty-Two

I turn to Thorn. "I'm going to the door. Maybe Isabella's mom is there, and they are doing something together, but I can't shake the feeling something's wrong."

Thorn opens the truck door. "I'll go with you."

We walk around the house to the front of the small, gray-shingled house. Two large cement blocks serve as steps to the low wooden porch.

Thorn grabs my arm. "Careful where you step. Some of these boards are rotted."

I understand. Our porch is the same. A screen door, missing its screen, hangs crookedly from the doorframe. I carefully pull it open and knock on the wooden front door. There's no sound in the house, no footsteps coming to the door. A chill runs up my spine. I knock with urgency. "Isabella? Are you in there? Open the door if you're here."

A slight sound hangs in the air. I turn to Thorn. "Did you hear something? Like maybe a whimper?"

"No." Thorn shakes his head. "Nothing."

Is it just my own past abuse feeding my imagination? My own whimpers echoing through the years? I shake my head. No, I'm sure I heard something. I knock again louder. "Isabella, open up."

A sound catches my ear, and I turn toward the voice. A lady is on a nearby front porch watching us. "Ain't no one there. The mama works late, and the little girl goes to after-school care. Sometimes she goes to a sitter's house if the mama works late. They ain't home yet"

I turn to Thorn. "I know I heard something in there. We have to get help."

"What do you want to do? Call 911? Break a window and go in?"

I think about it. "I don't want to leave and risk Isabella suffering more, but we have to do this right, or he'll get away with it. We need someone who will really listen to us."

"Okay," he agrees. We head to the alley and climb into his truck, and Thorn backs out.

I turn to him. "Let's go back to the church. We'll make someone listen."

"Coach will listen, especially if you tell him who your grandfather is. Remember, your grandfather is the reason Coach left in the first place."

Thorn is right. But that doesn't make it any easier when we get to the church. Coach is teaching the middle-school group how to do wall spins. He straightens up to stare at us as we rush in, then instructs the kids to take turns trying the skill. He then walks over. "Is anything wrong?"

I nod. The words are stuck in my throat.

He crossed his arms across his chest. "Does this have anything to do with why you weren't going to come tonight?"

"Yes. I … it's my grandfather … He used to … hurt me." I hate the quiver in my voice. I've never talked to anyone but Thorn and Mom about my grandfather's abuse.

Coach is looking at me. He doesn't get it.

"He … you know, hurt me … in a way grandfathers aren't supposed to hurt little girls."

I look into his eyes, willing him to understand. I can't give details. I see the realization of what I've said cross his face. His expression is a mix of shock and disgust. I hope it's toward my grandfather, not me. It must be. He would know it wasn't my fault.

Thorn cuts in. "You used to work for her grandfather, Walter Scott. He's been volunteering here. He's been watching you coach our team and work with the kids here. When he told her mom that you were here, her mom said she couldn't come anymore."

Coach's eyes are wide. "Melonie Scott is your mother?"

"Yes. But that's not important. I think my grandfather is hurting one of the little girls in the after-school program. Just like he did me."

"Molesting her?"

Heat floods my face. How can he say it so easily? I've never been able to choke out the word. I nod. "Yes. He's at her house now. He might have just taken her home, but I doubt it. I knocked on the door. No one answered, but I think I heard a whimper."

"You're sure he's in the house? And the mother isn't?"

"If her mom is there, why wouldn't she answer? I knocked and called Isabella's name loud enough that a neighbor came out. Besides, we found some stuff online about him."

Coach rubs his hands together, then clenches his fists. "Let me find someone to take this group. Carolyn leaves as soon as the after-school kids are gone, but the assistant director is here somewhere. The older kids can have open gym tonight, and I'll go with you. There is no one I trust less than Walter Scott."

I head to Thorn's truck with Thorn and Coach just behind me, when Mom pulls to the curb. She jumps out of the car and faces me. "I knew you'd be here. I told you to stay away from him." She points at Coach. "He's no good. You get in the car now."

"Mom. Your dad is hurting a little girl. We have to go."

She looks at me. "What are you talking about? How can he be hurting a girl? Isn't he here with you?"

I shake my head. "No, he's not. And I found evidence in his room. We can talk about this later. We have to go."

She looks from me to Coach, then turns her back on him and faces me. "You're sure? You're not just saying this because of what he did to you?"

"He's in her house and wouldn't answer when I knocked. I heard a whimper. We have to go." Why won't she listen? Tears spill down my face. "You can keep believing what you want, but I AM going to stop this. I don't care what I have to do."

I turn and run to Thorn's truck, yank the door open, and climb in. Thorn jumps in and pulls out, flooring the vehicle. We speed through the streets back to Isabella's house. As we pull up to the curb, Coach and my mom are right behind us. Coach jumps the steps and lands on the porch, the rest of us hurrying behind him. He strides to the door and knocks. "Isabella?"

A door slams at the back of the house. I jump the steps and

race around the house. My grandfather is running toward his car with Isabella—bundled into a bright-red, too-large parka—slung over his shoulder. All I can see is her tangled hair and wide brown eyes, filled with confusion and fear. My anger burns. I spring into action, racing toward them. "Stop!"

Isabella lets out a wail, her eyes widening with terror as she catches sight of me. Is she pleading for my help, or has my grandfather convinced her that I'm the enemy here? My grandfather ignores me completely as he yanks open his car door, effortlessly tosses Isabella into the back seat, then climbs into the driver's seat, slamming the door. He starts the car and maneuvers around the bushes.

"Don't let him get away," I yell to Thorn and Coach as they sprint past me. "He has Isabella!"

Chapter Twenty-Three

Thorn races across the yard as my grandfather backs into the alley and speeds away, knocking over two large trashcans. I follow Thorn as he runs after my grandfather's car, vaulting over the fallen trashcans. I land in the alley behind Thorn, but my grandfather is too far ahead. The only reason he's not out of sight is because he's slowed by debris alongside the alley. He maneuvers around an old toilet fixture, several large paint buckets, and some fallen fencing. For once, I'm glad for rubbish.

I race down the alley and catch up with Thorn. We sprint side by side. My grandfather hits a trashcan and sends it rolling right at us, the stench of rotted food assaulting my nose. I jump over the can and keep going without breaking my stride.

Coach looks back at us. "We have to get ahead of him to stop him."

"How?" Thorn calls.

Coach slows down just enough for us to catch up with him. He isn't even breathing hard as he continues explaining at a full sprint. "I know this area. In a couple more blocks, the alley dead-ends. He'll have to turn right onto a side street. There's an old playground that used to be part of a daycare just ahead where we can cut him off."

Sure enough, when we reach the next corner, off to the right there's an overgrown lot that holds a small, dilapidated building and rusted playground equipment. Coach is already vaulting over the chain-link fence that surrounds the abandoned daycare. Thorn and I hit the fence right behind him.

The equipment is broken, chains hanging empty from a swing set. We sprint toward the far side of the playground, jump over a fallen slide, and keep going. There's a bench ahead. Coach goes over first. Thorns goes next, and I follow, placing my left hand on the bench back and swinging my legs over. The fence is half pushed over on our side. We run up it, jump, and keep going.

Coach turns to me. "He should be hitting the dead-end about now." But even as Coach says it, we see the silver car racing down the side street. We're too late!

Coach and Thorn sprint even faster, and I try to keep up. Why didn't I push harder at track? My lungs burn as I gasp for air. I can't keep up. I slow, sucking in air.

A familiar car catches my eye. Mom is driving down the street parallel to the alley! She pulls across the side road and stops. The sound of screeching brakes fills the air. My grandfather's car spins sideways and comes to a stop inches from Mom's passenger door. I dash to catch up with Coach and Thorn.

My grandfather's eyes narrow as he spots Coach, Thorn, and me closing in on him. I rush to the passenger side and yank on the door handle. Locked!

Coach punches in 9-1-1 and speaks into the phone, giving them our location. He looks around, then picks up a large rock. With his jaw clenched, he looks like someone I wouldn't want to tangle with. "Open the door, or I'll bust your window."

My grandfather opens the door and steps out of the car, locking Isabella in. He drops the keys into his pocket. His face is a mask. No fear. Nothing. "Come now. I don't know what my emotionally unstable granddaughter has been telling you, but there is clearly some misunderstanding here.

Heat rushes through me like an overflowing river, and my words come rushing out. "There's no misunderstanding. You were going to molest her." I've said the word. "And this time you aren't going to get away with it, because we've found proof. We have the record of your arrest for doing the very same thing in Montgomery, Alabama."

I step toward the car. Isabella, confused and fearful, is peering out at me. She's fumbling at the door, trying to open it. I have no doubt my grandfather has the child safety lock on, so it won't open from the inside. I reach for the door myself and yank on it. It won't budge.

"Let her out!" I yell.

My grandfather pushes me away from the car door, then blocks it with his body. "You think I'm going to let you anywhere near that child, crazy as you've been acting? As it is, since I haven't been able to contact her mother, I'm going to drive her straight to the police station and explain how you and your lunatic boyfriend—" He glares over at Thorn—"tried to break in and attack her. She's already scared enough of you from your outbursts at church. As I'm sure the director of the after-school program, where I'm a valued volunteer, will be happy to testify."

My mouth has dropped open as I stare at my grandfather. In my silence, he keeps speaking in hard, ugly phrases. "As to Montgomery, if you've been so thorough, you should know that silly little incident was completely dismissed. A greedy, single mother, tired of living off taxpayers, figures she can cash in by accusing me, an upstanding business owner and philanthropist. Her own daughter made it amply clear to the police that her mother was an angry drunk, and I'd been nothing but kind to her— as Isabella undoubtedly will also."

My blood goes cold at his words. They are so measured, rational, and believable. I counter, "Then explain why you left Montgomery. Sure looks like you were running from an investigation there."

"I decided to retire," my grandfather responds coldly. "Car sales were in freefall, and I deserved to start taking some time for myself. As to moving, why should I stay around such a group of ingrates when there are plenty of less fortunate people elsewhere needing the help of good people like myself."

"That's not why you moved and kept moving. You know it, and I know it! And the police will know exactly what you are when I explain how ..."

My grandfather spins around and leans in close, anger deeply etched into his face. The mask is gone. His mouth turns to a sneer. "You shut up! You think anyone would believe you over me? You're nothing but a mongrel."

Coach steps forward to my side and faces my grandfather. "That's enough of your filthy talk."

He grabs a broken brick from the ground, then pushes past my grandfather to address Isabella through the car window. "Cover your face with your coat."

The fury on my grandfather's face deepens, but he has enough sense to know he can't prevail against Coach's superior strength. He reluctantly steps away as Coach smashes the window with the rock, unlocks and opens the door. He carefully lifts Isabella out. Still confused and fearful, she reaches out her arms toward my grandfather, then catches sight of his furious expression and buries her face against Coach's shirt.

I turn to my grandfather, resuming the conversation. "What right do you have to call me a mongrel? After what you did to me, you're nothing but a monster. And maybe I was too small and afraid back then to speak up about it, but not anymore. Once I tell my own story, it won't matter what lies you tell about Isabella. It'll be over for you."

"On the contrary," my grandfather says, "I'm sure the police will understand why I was driving her to the police station. And as for you—"

My grandfather pauses. I stare at him, wondering if he's going to keep up the lie right to my face. Then, as though he can't keep in his real self anymore, he leans in even closer to me and hisses so that I can feel the spittle on my face, "As for you, you filthy little mongrel, anything I did, you deserved. You were a constant reminder of what that man did to your mother, my beautiful princess. I walked in on them, you know. They were in my office at the car lot on graduation night. Your mom and ... him!"

My grandfather gestures towards Coach Jones, the ugliness of prejudice lining his face. "By the time I found them, she'd ruined herself with him."

I glance toward Coach Jones, expecting some kind of explosive reaction to my grandfather's words, but he has stepped back a few feet with Isabella. He is whispering soothingly in her ear, trying to shield her from my grandfather's foul words.

Instead, it's Mother who steps forward, placing herself in front of me, toe to toe with my grandfather. "I loved Terrence. If you hadn't been so intolerant, we could have had a real relationship."

Red creeps up my grandfather's face. "You? My only daughter?

With a n—"

Mom pokes him in the chest, jabbing him as each word comes from her mouth. "Don't you say it! Don't you dare!"

My grandfather's face tinges red, and his eyes bulge. Once again, his fury is so great he can't rein it in with his usual charm and lies. "That trash took you from me, spoiled my beautiful little girl. And believe me, I made sure he paid for it, and that it would never happen again. When I found you together, I knew I had to get rid of him. Being what he is ..." The sneer deepens on his face, contempt and hate dripping like acid from his lips. "I knew the police would believe me, one of the town's most respected businessmen, not to mention a taxpayer who funded their salaries, over some delinquent from the Mill District."

Mom is in shock. "You mean, you're the one who put the money in his car that day? There was never a theft?" She spins around to Coach. "Why did you confess to me that you stole it? Why?"

The calmness flees Coach's face as he raises his head, burying Isabella even tighter against his chest. A wave of something replaces it. Pain? No, more than that, deep grief, maybe even anguish. Then he straightens up, his usual calm restored.

He rubs a hand across his mouth and chin and just looks at Mom. I drop my own eyes at the intensity of his gaze. This is between the two of them. Coach finally speaks. "He said if I didn't leave and promise to never see you again, he'd press charges. Like he said, who would they believe? A businessman or a black teen from the mill district? Since your father knew if I told you the truth of what he'd done, you'd take my side, so part of the deal was me confessing to you I had stolen the money. And since I wouldn't be seeing you again, I came to believe it really was better if you thought the worst of me, so you'd let me go and get on with your own life. Go to college and make something of yourself."

Mom's mouth is still wide open. She snaps it shut. "You ... you ... That wasn't your choice! You shouldn't have lied to me!" Her words are like bricks. I'm glad they aren't aimed at me.

Coach stuffs his fists in his pockets. "Later on, I wanted to come back and find you. Especially since I'd learned by then about something called the statute of limitations, so whatever so-called evidence your grandfather might try to hold over me—too much time had passed for him to file charges against me. But then I heard you had a kid and figured you'd gotten married and moved on.

Coach glances over at me. "I guess I was right about the moving on, at least."

By now, I have raised my head, looking from Coach's face to my mother's. I can't quite read her expression. Anger? Regret? Shame?

Then my grandfather takes a menacing step toward Coach, pushing my mom behind him. "You think I'd have ever let you back near my daughter? I would have done whatever it took to keep you apart, including making sure you ended up in prison if you ever dared touch her again."

Coach gives a perplexed shake of his head. "I just don't get it. Melonie and I shouldn't have done what we did that night. But it wasn't something casual either. We loved each other. Wanted to get married after graduation. Spend the rest of our lives together. That you would go to these lengths over a wrong action a lot of young couples have done—well, that is what didn't make sense then and still doesn't now."

I hadn't thought my grandfather's face could get redder and more distended. "You don't get it? You think this is about that night? What it was about was the nerve you had of ever dreaming you were good enough to touch my daughter, much less marry her. If you had, believe me, you wouldn't just be in prison. As it was, I never would have let you skip town if I'd had any idea then ..."

Something changes in Coach's expression as my grandfather trails off, like gears turning and meshing or like an algebra problem finally making sense. But he speaks calmly. "If you hated me so much, why did you hire me in the first place?"

"You were a good worker," my grandfather sneers. "Good with your hands and good with numbers. Not to mention willing to work for minimum wage. But that was your place, working for me. Not defiling my daughter! And certainly not getting her pregnant!"

At this moment, the universe stops. Not a sound breaks the

silence, not even Isabella as she stares at her white-haired friend, thankfully not understanding what is going on. I can't even breathe as the realization of what my grandfather has said sinks in. I stare at Mom, waiting for her to correct him, but she and Terrence are staring at each other.

Coach is the first to break the silence. Still looking at Mom, he asks, "Kiana is my daughter? Why didn't you tell me, Melonie? You have to know if I had any idea your child was mine, I would have been here in a heartbeat. I would have made it right. We'd have been a family."

Mom's voice quivers. "How could I tell you? You told me you were a thief. That you'd never really loved me. You broke my heart! I never got over it … or over you."

"It broke my heart too, but I really thought I was doing the right thing for you … that you were happy with someone else."

My gut clenches at seeing the unmistakable pain on Coach's face. What this bombshell means to me, I haven't even begun to process. It's enough to know I wasn't wrong in trusting him. He really is good, kind, honest, and all the other things to me and to the other kids at school and church.

Coach's expression suddenly goes stern, his gaze deepening in intensity as he studies Mom's face. "We can blame each other all day, Melonie. And maybe there will be a right time to talk it all out. But we were just a couple of dumb kids in love. There's only one person really responsible for all this. I hope you see that now."

"I do." A tear trickles down Mom's face. She's always seemed careworn, made older than her age by her bad choices, but at this moment, she looks as young, confused, and frightened as Isabella. For the first time, I can see that pretty, carefree cheerleader, crazy in love with the cutest track star in the school. "And I'm sure he knows now."

Mom turns toward her father with a look of pleading. "Dad, come on. You don't mean all this ugly talk. I know you're sorry for what you did to Kiana and to Terrence. Right? You just don't know how to say it."

My grandfather's face is livid. "I did nothing to be sorry for."

Mom shrinks back as though slapped. 'You don't really mean

that." It sounds more like pleading than a statement. I want to go to her side. To tell her it will be okay. But my feet won't move, and it won't be okay.

Coach holds Isabella close in one arm, then reaches out and pulls Mom away from her father with the other. His jaw tightens, and his words are clipped. "He doesn't know how to feel remorse."

Mom looks up at him. "All this time. All Kiana and I have been through. All because my father couldn't stand the thought of me with you." She drops her head to his shoulder and leans into him. I wish he'd reach out and pull me in too, but I'm okay. Mom needs him more.

Thorn is standing close. He must sense my feelings because he reaches out and pulls me back so I'm leaning against him. The distant sound of a siren fills the air. Then another. Mom lifts her head and steps back from Coach.

My grandfather has heard the sirens too. As he turns his head toward them, Coach speaks up again, colder than I've ever heard his voice. "It's over. Isabella or not, there are four of us here to give testimony against you. And believe me, we will. Right, Melonie?"

Mom's nod is tentative, but unmistakable. My grandfather should be looking more worried than he is. He sneers, "It's still the word of a bunch of losers against me. My alcoholic daughter who can't keep a job and two unstable delinquents. As for you, Terrence, by time I get done, you'll never coach again. In fact, you'll wish you'd never set foot back in this town. Your so-called celebrity status will mean nothing."

"Not quite just our word." It was the first time Thorn had spoken up, and my grandfather looked startled by the harshness in Thorn's voice. He releases me and holds up his phone. "It's just a cheap minutes phone, but it takes great video, and I've been using it to record this conversation. You know, just in case anyone decides to deny what was said later." He grins. "I think the police will find it quite interesting."

The sirens are much louder now, and I see flashing blue lights just blocks away. Panic floods my grandfather's face. For the first time in his life, he realizes there is no lying or charming his way out of a situation. But he's not ready to give up yet. In a sudden move, he barrels forward, shoving me back against Thorn. By the time we've regained our balance, he has Thorn's phone.

Chapter Twenty-Four

Coach springs forward, but he's still carrying Isabella, and Mom is in his way. As he hands Isabella to Mom, my grandfather is already opening his car door. Half falling into the driver's seat, he turns on the engine while simultaneously yanking the car door shut. Coach reaches him just as he accelerates, scraping against Mom's car where she'd parked diagonally across the road to block him in. He clips her front bumper with enough force to knock her car out of his path.

But Coach isn't giving up. As my grandfather brakes hard to take the corner at a tight skid that heads him away from the approaching sirens, Coach sprints diagonally to intercept the car. He leaps, landing on the rear end of the silver convertible. My grandfather swerves back and forth trying to unbalance Coach. Despite the circumstances, I almost grin. Not going to happen.

The car accelerates, still weaving back and forth in a tight Z. I gasp as Coach loses his grip and is thrown off the convertible, but he manages to hit the ground in a tight roll. He comes up in a crouch, facing the accelerating convertible. I tamp down mingled relief and frustration as I race toward him with Thorn keeping pace beside me. Frustration my grandfather has once again—unbelievably, infuriatingly—managed to escape floods through me, along with anger that he has Thorn's phone, our only real evidence. Yet I'm relieved that Coach seems to be okay, though scraped and bruised.

No, not Coach. My father. My father! The thought almost makes up for the disappointment of my grandfather's getaway. Thorn and I stop as we get to my father, who is now pushing himself to his feet.

That is when we hear above the blasting sirens the sound of crumpling metal and shattering glass. Stunned, I look up to see the red taillights now slanted at a diagonal, perhaps a hundred meters ahead. I am sure I beat my own record for the 100-meter dash by the time I reach my grandfather's car. Coach and Thorn are already there.

The front of the convertible is so crumpled the headlights are not working, but in the dim of the red taillights, I can make out what has happened. My grandfather was clearly not able to pull out of that last zig-zag when he'd thrown Coach free and accelerated straight into a broken, useless street light.

My grandfather is slumped over the wheel, his airbag already deflating. Glass from the broken windshield is embedded in his head, and blood trickles from the wound.

Coach? Dad? Terrence?—I settle mentally on Coach since that's how I usually think of him—yanks on the driver's door, but it won't open. People from surrounding houses are starting to arrive, staying far enough back to be out of the way but straining to see what's happened. Flashing blue lights fill the street, and two police cars pull up by my grandfather's car.

Four officers get out and surround the car. One tries to open the driver's door, but it won't budge. My grandfather is too wedged in to get him out through any other door. The officer reaches inside his police car and talks on the radio. Minutes later, a fire truck and ambulance screech to a halt beside the police cars.

A fireman uses a bar to force the door open. The paramedics roll a stretcher to the car, and the fireman and a paramedic lift my grandfather out of the car and onto the stretcher. He is limp and unmoving, blood spattering his face and shirt. I can't see more than that. I should feel something, but I don't. It's like it's all happening to someone else.

I walk back to find Mom. She is sitting on the sidewalk, cradling Isabella in her arms. While the crash is far enough down the street that she probably doesn't know what happened, the lights and sirens are scaring her. Mom tries to comfort her, but Isabella continues to cry.

Mom looks up at me. "How is your grandfather?"

"He's alive. They're taking him to the hospital." I drop down by Mom.

"I'm wondering what to do about Isabella. If her mom's still not home, I don't know whether to take her back to the church, keep her with us, or what. I don't want her to have to go to the police station or social services or somewhere that would scare her," I say.

"Let's just wait here for Terrence. He'll know what to do."

"You were pretty cool tonight. What made you think to cut grandpa off with your car?"

Mom slumped her shoulders. "I don't know, but I thought if I could catch him maybe ..."

"Maybe what?"

"Maybe it would help make up for my not calling the police years ago."

She needs me to say it's okay, but right now it's not. Not yet, at least. Still, she lost as much because of her dad as I did. I give a little nod and reach for Isabella. "Why don't you go see what's going on with Coach and your dad."

I settle Isabella on my lap, and she looks up at me, "I want my mommy. And I want my grandpa friend. Where did he go? He was going to take me for ice cream if I played a game with him. Then you showed up, and he said we had to leave. I was going to yell at you to leave, but he putted his hand over my mouth."

So that's the whimper I heard. Not one of fear, but because he kept her from yelling at me. I guess you don't always get thanks for being the hero. But maybe it's better that she will never know what might have happened to her. Still, someone needs to warn these kids about people like my grandfather. Isabella starts to whimper. I pull my Statue of Liberty coin from my pocket and rub it between my thumb and first finger.

Isabella stops whimpering. "What's that thing you have?"

"It's something special I always carry. It gives me something to hold when I feel worried or upset." I open my hand so she can see it. "Would you like it?"

Isabella reaches out to take it, then closes her small hand around it.

Mom is walking back toward me with Coach and Thorn. When they reach me, Mom digs her car keys from her pocket. "A tow truck will be here to take both your grandfather's car and mine."

I glance toward the cars. I'd forgotten all about the damage to Mom's car.

She continues, "I'm going with my father in the ambulance. You and Thorn can go with Terrence back to Isabella's house to pick up the other vehicles. Then Terrence is going to bring you to the hospital."

It doesn't seem I'm being offered any choice here, so I remain silent. Isabella shifts on my lap, taking in the scene with wide eyes. She's rubbing the coin between her two hands. Mom looks at her. "Hopefully, her mom is home by now, so you can leave her there."

Mom walks over to the ambulance and climbs in the back. The ambulance pulls away just as a tow truck arrives. While the driver starts pulling chains from the back, a police officer heads toward us. Coach steps out to meet him. After a short conversation, Coach and the officer approach us. Coach looks at Thorn, Isabella, and me with compassion-filled eyes. "They've recovered Thorn's phone in the car and have seen the video. But we still all need to give statements, and that means going to the police station before we head to the hospital. Are you two okay with that?"

I sigh. I just want today to be over. I want things to go back to the way they were. No, I want things to be better than they were. But Thorn is right. Before things can get better, I have to face them. At least now it will be easier to talk about what happened. My grandfather has finally shown everyone what he really is. I clench my jaw. I can do this.

Coach stoops to lift Isabella from my lap. "First, the police officer has agreed that getting Isabella home is a priority."

A female police officer has now joined us. "I'm going to give you a ride home in my car with the pretty blue lights. Won't that be fun?"

Isabella looks up with big brown eyes. "I never got my ice cream with the nice man. I'm hungry."

I smile. Isabella is going to be okay. Even if she never realizes what I did for her, it's okay. I know that I've saved her from memories that would haunt her for years to come.

The other police officer gestures us toward his own vehicle.

"We haven't forgotten the 9-1-1 call that started all this. The officer with Isabella will get her account of things, but it's your stories we want to hear. We'll do this properly at the police station."

Thankfully, the time at the police station goes quickly. I thought they'd hear our stories together, but instead Coach, Thorn, and I are led off separately. I find myself in an interrogation room as they call it on TV—just a small room with a table, chairs, and a mirror. I'm pretty sure it's the kind you can see through from the other side.

The police officer we have come with sits across from me, along with another officer I haven't seen before. He turns on a recorder. "Why don't you just start at the beginning. What led up to tonight's crash and the 9-1-1 call about a child being kidnapped?"

I nod. "I'll start with what my grandfather did to me, which is why I suspected him when I saw him doing the same things with Isabella."

I give them the short version of my own story, trying to show no emotion and hoping that telling it will ensure my grandfather can never hurt another person. Then I tell them everything that happened these last weeks, starting with my grandfather taking Isabella to the bathroom to clean her shirt and ending with what we found online.

After we all give our reports, the police officer drives us back to where we left Thorn's truck and Coach's car. At least the police interrogation saved us the hike back from the abandoned playground. Lights are on in Isabella's house when we arrive. As we step out, I hear a woman's voice followed by a little girl's laughter. Yes, Isabella is going to be okay.

Next, we head to the church. I ride with Thorn so Coach can fill in the assistant program director and make sure the kids are taken care of. I wait in Thorn's truck while Coach goes inside.

"I feel like I should be going with you to the hospital, but I promised Grandpa to help him load the supplies he'll need for a job first thing tomorrow morning. Still, if you want me to come, just say so. I'm sure Grandpa would understand."

"I'll be okay." I scoot across the seat and hug him, letting myself lean against him until Coach comes back out. I follow him to his black Ford Edge. He unlocks and opens the passenger door for me. I've ridden with him before, but this time it's different because before he was Coach, and now he's Dad. And I don't even know what to do with that.

Chapter Twenty-Five

An awkward silence fills the car as Coach eases out of the church parking lot. I wrap my arms around myself and lean against the door.

Coach turns toward me. "I don't know where to start or what to say to you. I'm ... well, I guess I'm still in a bit of shock."

"Me too. You're like the missing piece to the puzzle of my life. I just ... I can't seem to wrap my mind around it."

He nods. "You do have an advantage, though. You knew you had a dad somewhere. I never in a million years imagined I had a daughter."

"True."

We sit quietly, then he breaks the silence. "Maybe I can fill in some of the other missing pieces for you."

"About?"

"About your mom and me."

I nod.

"I'll start with high school. You know Cassandra Clark, Melonie ... your mom, I mean ... and I all went to school together. Cassandra and I both ran track. I think you know that already."

I nod again.

"That meant we spent a lot of time together. We both lived in the poor section. We were on the bus together, at school together, at track together. People started thinking of us as a couple."

I turn toward him. "Were you?"

He sighs. "For a while. Since everyone thought we were together, I took her to homecoming our senior year."

Coach Jones and Coach Clark? They are too different. I look at him and realize he's waiting for me to say something. I shake my head. "I can't picture that."

"Well, let's just say it didn't work out. She took our

relationship a lot more seriously than I did." He stops for a red light, then turns down Eighth Street.

"So, you broke up?"

He nods. "I did. And it wasn't pretty. I won't go into details. I turned my focus to work, which you already know was at your grandfather's car lot. I was saving to go to college."

Coach turns into the hospital parking lot, pulls into a space, turns his car off, but doesn't get out. "Your mom worked for her dad sometimes on weekends. But when he wasn't there—like out on a test drive with a customer— we'd talk. I thought she was really great. Upbeat and fun to talk to. She liked me too. Must have been my charm and good looks." He grins, but it fades. "I knew I had no hope of dating her. You heard how your grandfather talked about me." His voice breaks. He starts to say something, then just shakes his head. Silence fills the car.

"What?"

He shakes his head. "If only I could go back and do things over. Save you from what you went through."

I don't know what to say, so I open the door and climb out. He does the same. I try to shut down the conflicting emotions threatening to overtake me.

We enter the emergency room where Mom is waiting.

"How is he?" Coach asks.

"They are still checking him over," Mom says. "He has a concussion and internal injuries, but they don't know yet how bad it is."

I scowl. "But he'll go to jail or something now, right? For what he tried to do?"

"The police are up there. He'll be charged," Mom said.

I should say something, but nothing comes to mind. "Can I go home now? It's been a long day."

Mom's shoulders slump. "I know. I want to leave too, but I need to stay at least long enough to talk to his doctor. Despite everything, he is my father."

"I can take her home and stay with her," Coach says.

"I'm fifteen. I don't need a babysitter."

"I'm not a babysitter, I'm your coach—and your father."

His words startle me. I know he's my father, but until now it hadn't occurred to me that anything about my life might change because of that.

"Kiana?"

I look up. Coach is watching me.

"What?"

"What were you just thinking?"

I shrug. "Nothing."

He laughs. "The look on your face makes that hard to believe, but you don't have to tell me."

"This is all too weird for me. You and Mom together. The fact you're my father. My grandfather and the chase scene that just happened. I'm waiting for the lights to go on and the movie to be over."

"Do you want to talk about it?" Coach asks. He glances over at my mom. "Both of you?"

Now I feel really awkward. "What else is there to say?"

"Well, maybe it's time for your mom and me to do the talking." Coach leads us to a corner where oversized chairs are arranged in a circle. "Why don't we sit down?"

After we get comfortable, Coach asks, "So, Kiana, what do you need to know? Besides what I already told you in the car."

I shrug. "I think I pretty well got the picture from the nasty stuff Grandpa said."

Mom looks at me. "That was his point of view. Terrence and I were drawn to each other. I fell in love with him, but your grandfather never would have heard of us seeing each other." She glances sideways at Coach, but he doesn't say anything. "On graduation night, Terrence and I met at my grandfather's car dealership. I can't really make excuses for what happened, but we were both excited about graduation, and our emotions were running high."

"Why couldn't you wait until you were away from Grandpa? I mean, you could have gone away to college together or something."

"That's just what we did plan," Coach answers seriously. "We had both planned on going to Alabama, away from her parents. To start our relationship there. But we acted impulsively, and everything came crashing down. I went from graduation to being with your mom, and then to jail." He stops and stares at his hands, then looks up at me. "Your grandfather came to see me. Like you heard earlier, he said if I'd promise not to ever contact your mom again, he'd drop the charges. I agreed and was freed."

Mom interrupts. "But I didn't know. My dad came home and told me Terrence had admitted to stealing from him. He pretended to be hurt by Terrence's 'betrayal' of his trust. He told me Terrence had used me to get into the office and take the money. I didn't want to believe it, so I snuck out and called Terrence. He told me it was true and that he was leaving."

I turn to look at Coach. "I still don't see why you couldn't have just told her the truth, even if it meant both of you leaving town together. If you had, maybe we'd have been a family all these years. Grandpa would never have ..."

As I break off, Coach slams his palms down on his legs. "Like I said earlier, I thought it would be better for her. If I said I did it, she'd turn away from me, and then her father could give her the life she deserved. If I hadn't, he could have ruined us both. Remember, we weren't much older than you are now, Kiana—barely eighteen. What could we do against him?"

I have no answer since I'm hardly an example of standing up against my grandfather. I can't really wrap my mind around what I'd do if I'd been in their place.

Coach looks sadly at my mom. "I wish I'd known you were pregnant, Melonie. I'd have moved heaven and earth to get you out of there and make us a family."

His voice chokes. He swallows twice and tries to speak, but no words come out. He drops his elbows to his knees and clasps his hands, looking down at the floor and shaking his head. He doesn't need words. I know exactly what he means.

I clear my throat. "All those years of just Mom and me. Of my grandfather's abuse ..."

He straightens up. "I know ..."

"You missed the first fifteen years of my life. If you'd been here I could have had a normal life."

I inhale and let the air fill me. I blink several times, and bite back a sob. I'm not going to make a scene. I stand and start to walk away, but Coach stands and pulls me against him. I put my hands flat on his chest and half-heartedly try to push him away, but he just pulls me tighter. I give up, bury my face in his shirt, and allow the tears flow.

His warmth spreads to me. I feel some of my pain fading away. He puts his mouth to my ear. "I'm so sorry."

It's a whisper, but I hear it. It makes my heart do funny things. I wrap my arms around him and sigh. Is this what it feels like to have a dad? To be a daughter?

I might have asked him. Which is silly since, like Coach said, he has no more experience at being a dad than I do being his daughter. Just then, a nurse walks up to us, shattering the moment. She addresses Mom.

"Your father is awake. He's in a lot of pain, and the doctor has left a sedative to help him rest, but he insists on seeing his family first, if you'd like to come with me."

Grandpa's asking to see us? Why, after our last extremely unpleasant confrontation? Maybe his injuries are worse than the nurse is letting on, and he wants to make things right in case he dies.

Maybe even to apologize to his granddaughter?

Chapter Twenty-Six

A police officer is standing outside my grandfather's room in the intensive care unit, indicating that he isn't a normal hospital patient. I tag along reluctantly behind Mom and Coach as they follow the nurse into his room.

My grandfather is stretched out under a blanket on a hospital bed, but the end where his head rests is raised at an angle so that he is half sitting. Clear liquids flow from an IV bag into his arm. He has bandages on his head and around his face where the windshield glass cut him. Bruises around his eyes are already darkening from yellow-and-green to black-and-blue.

He doesn't look like he's on his deathbed or in any way apologetic. His chill gaze shifts from Coach and Mom to me as he addresses the nurse. "Get out. I want to speak to my family alone."

As the nurse closes the door after her, he turns his glare on Coach. "You too!"

"I'm not leaving them," Coach responds calmly. "They are my family too."

"Your family!" my grandfather explodes. "Over my dead body. And believe me, I'm nowhere near that yet."

Mom steps forward. "Dad, don't be like this. We're all here for you."

"Here for me? When you're trying to have me thrown into prison?" His face twists with anger. "The only thing I want from any of you is to tell those police officers this was all a mistake. Tell them your boyfriend ..." He shakes his finger at me, making the word sound like something dirty, "cobbled together his recording, and it was taken completely out of context."

"I'll never do that! You belong in prison!" The words burst from my mouth before I know I'm going to say them. "And that's where you're going. To pay for what you did to me and who knows how many other little girls who were your victims but never got justice.”

“You! You are nothing but a mongrel!” My grandfather struggles to sit up but falls back. He’s so worked up, spittle appears around his mouth. I want to gag. “You were never my true granddaughter. Not with the likes of him mixed with my pure DNA.”

The depth of his prejudice silences anything I might have said. Coach takes a step forward, but Mom puts a hand on his arm. I regain my voice. “For someone who despises my heritage, you sure seem to have a liking for little girls who share it.”

My grandfather’s face twists with a mixture of pain and anger. “What difference does it make to someone like you? You think you deserve any better treatment? I suppose you’re thrilled to have that for your dad.” He nods toward Coach, then sinks back, his face pale with pain.

I’m ready to retort when the nurse reenters the room, carrying a small tray with a pill and water in a paper cup. She glances at us, standing tensely by my grandfather’s bed. “It seems you are getting my patient worked up. I think it’s time for you to leave so he can take his sedative and get some rest.”

I don’t need any further invitation to leave. I push past her at a run. If Mom was hoping for reconciliation, she’s out of luck. He’s made it clear, in his mind, Coach and I are nothing but trash.

Mom and Coach follow me out of my grandfather’s room. When I stop, they catch up with me. I feel exhausted as the day’s events flood back over me. Finding my grandfather at Isabella’s house. The chase. The crash. It all washes over me. “I need to get out of here,” I announce.

Coach steps forward to put his arm around my shoulder, looking over at my mom. “Melonie, why don’t I take her to get something to eat? We could bring something back for you if you’re going to stay to talk to the doctor. Or, we can all go, and I’ll bring you back to check on your father later.”

“I’ll stay. You take Kiana. She needs to eat. I’m fine.”

I follow Coach outside to his car. As he pulls out of the parking lot, he looks over at me. “Pizza okay? I could show you one of my favorite places.”

I nod. He maneuvers through the hospital zone, then takes the highway to Front Beach Road where white sand and the ocean line one side of the road, and a row of small specialty shops line the other. Coach pulls off at a small, white building marked by a driftwood sign that reads “Beachside Pizza.”

Coach walks around and opens my door. I slowly climb out. He looks at me. “This isn’t going to be awkward, is it? We’ve spent time together before.”

I bite my lower lip. “That was when you were my track coach, not my dad.”

“I’m the same person.”

“Doesn’t feel the same.”

Coach holds the restaurant door open for me. The walls are white, and the tables are covered in red-checked cloths. Bottles of crushed red peppers and Parmesan sit side by side with napkin holders. He leads me to a table in the back corner. Sunlight streams in a large window. He picks up a brown leather menu. “What’s your favorite? Pepperoni? Ham?”

“Either.”

He looks at me. “Don’t be afraid to give your preference.”

“I guess I’m more in a ham mood. Maybe ham and pineapple.”

He orders and then turns to me. “Are you good with this?”

“With ham and pineapple?”

“No, with me as your dad.”

“I haven’t gotten used to the idea yet. I’m not sure how it’s going to work.”

His brows furrow. “What do you mean?”

I prop my elbows on the table and rest my chin in my hands, studying him. “Am I going to have visitation with you? Weekends? Two weeks in the summer? I’ve waited a long time for a dad, but I never expected one to show up. Now that you’re here, I don’t know what to expect. And what about track? Do we tell everyone you’re my dad or keep it a secret? Do I call you Dad when we’re out and Coach at school?”

He laughs. Embarrassment seeps in. I look into his face. “It’s not funny to me. I don’t know how these things work. I have no experience with having a dad."

He leans toward me. "I'm sorry. It's not funny. It's that I've never heard you say more than a few words at a time before, and that was a whole paragraph." He pauses, but I don't say anything. He continues. "I don't have the answers. One day, I'm a former winner of *Running Free* and a track coach. Next day, I have a teenage daughter. We'll have to figure it out as we go."

"What are you going to tell your family about me? They might not be too happy to find out you have a daughter."

He smiles. "Are you kidding? My mom will love having a granddaughter. Once she finds out about you, there will be no stopping her. Remember, she has two sons. Now she'll have a chance to spoil a granddaughter."

Coach tells me more about his family—my family now—until the pizza arrives. We are two slices in when my cell phone rings. "It's Mom."

"Give the phone to Terrence," she says.

"Why?" I ask.

"Just do it, Kiana. It's urgent."

I hand the phone to coach, and he listens intently. Then he signals our server. "We need a to-go box immediately."

Minutes later, box in hand, he leads me back out to his car, but the mood has changed. He pulls out onto the road and hits the gas.

"What's happened now?"

"Your grandfather's gone."

"Gone like dead or gone like missing?"

"Missing."

"Once the nurse gave your grandfather the sedative, the police officer outside the door thought it was safe to go for a cup of coffee. But it looks like he never really swallowed the sedative. And he must have been lying about how much pain he was in because when the officer got back, your grandfather was nowhere in sight."

My heart sinks as I remember my grandfather's angry vow that this wouldn't be the end for him. I don't know whether to be angry at myself for not suspecting him of trying something or at the police officer for not knowing better. I realize my hands are clenched into fists and force them to relax, but my stomach remains clenched. Whatever my grandfather is up to, it can't be good.

Chapter Twenty-Seven

We arrive back at the hospital to find it surrounded by police cars. Coach parks in the visitor lot, and we head for the hospital.

"Sorry, no one can enter right now," an officer says. "We're on lockdown."

"The missing man is her grandfather," Coach says.

The officer doesn't move. "You still need to stay out here and well away from the hospital. The missing man may be dangerous."

"You can't be serious," I respond. "He's an old man who's been in a car crash." My grandfather was certainly dangerous enough, but not in the way these officers were thinking. "Please, my mom is inside, and I need to get to her."

The officer's face was unyielding. "Anyone desperate to escape can become dangerous. We have officers searching the hospital right now. Once we get the all-clear, I'll get you to your mother."

I stand beside Coach. Where is Mom? And the bigger question—where is my grandfather?

A shout rings out. Police officers run to the front side of the hospital. One of the officers turns on a hand-held spotlight and shines it upward. My grandfather is perched on a ledge on the third story. How did he get there?"

"Go back into the building!" a voice orders from the police car closest to my grandfather.

My grandfather inches along the ledge. What is he doing? There's nowhere to go. Then, I spot the fire escape a few meters from where he is shuffling sideways. It suddenly makes sense. The intensive care unit is on the third floor. He must have snuck out once the police officer left. When the alarm sounded, he decided to climb through a window—maybe in an empty patient room—thinking he could dodge the hospital security by going down the fire escape.

As though reading my thoughts, Coach says, "He must have figured the security wouldn't be searching on the outside, at least not until they'd searched the hospital. But I don't like the way he's moving. If he's not careful, he's going to be over that ledge before he ever reaches the fire escape."

By now, my grandfather has stopped on the ledge. I can see why the police officers are pounding up the fire escape. One of them calls to my grandfather, "Just keep moving this way, sir. There's no other way down. Just keep moving, sir."

My grandfather is moving again, but now he's shuffling back the way he came. Another officer steps out of a window on the opposite side of the fire escape. A second officer follows.

"Go back toward the fire escape, sir!" a voice commands. "There's no other way down, and we don't want you hurting yourself."

Police officers are now inching toward my grandfather from both sides. My mouth goes dry. Honestly, I'm less worried about my grandfather than one of the officers. My grandfather stops again, unable to move left or right.

"Just stay where you are!" the voice orders.

The police officers are now close enough to reach for my grandfather, obviously trying to help him. What happens next is more of a blur. My grandfather shouts obscenities at the police officer, at the world, even at God himself. Then, flailing his arms, he tries to push the officers away. One police officer teeters dangerously toward the edge. His partners pull him back. My grandfather takes a swing at the officer and connects, but the momentum of that blow causes him to lose his balance. He teeters backward. I hear a loud shriek, then realize it's coming from me.

Coach spins me around to face him and pulls me tightly against his chest. The sound of a heavy thud hitting the pavement will haunt me for a long time. I pull away from Coach, run to some nearby bushes, and heave up my pizza. Then I drop to my knees, sobbing. Why am I crying? I hate my grandfather, don't I?

Strong arms lift me. "Let's get you home."

I struggle to get free. "I need to be here for Mom."

"It may be a long time before they let anyone in," he says.

"I'll wait."

While Coach goes to talk to an officer, I sit on a curb with my back turned away from the action taking place in front of the hospital. When he returns, he walks me around to a back entrance of the hospital where a security guard is waiting to let us in. I follow Coach down a hallway until he stops in front of a large door. When he opens it, I can see pews and a lectern at the front.

I follow Coach inside. "They have a church here?"

"It's a chapel. They have services here on Sundays, but mostly it's a quiet place to think and pray."

I shake my head. "I don't really have much to say to God."

Coach drops into a pew and slides over to make room for me. "That's okay. He has a lot to say to you."

"That sounds like something Thorn or his grandparents would say."

"They'd be right. What just happened outside was horrible. What happened to you years ago was also horrible. But it doesn't change the fact that God loves you and wants to be here for you. Nothing your grandfather did can change that."

"But now he's dead, and he never had to pay for what he did. I don't know how many little girls he hurt in all, but he should have had to pay."

"He will pay, Kiana. Just not in the way you want. Sure, he should have had to stand trial and go to prison, but the choice he just made is worse. He chose to leave this life unrepentant, cursing God even as he did so."

"And now he's free."

"No. He's not free. He will suffer God's judgment."

"I thought God loves everyone. He forgives everyone."

"He does love everyone. And he forgives those who ask. But your grandfather didn't. So, while he might escape prison here, what he will face in eternity is far worse."

I don't know what to say, so I just lean against my father and soak up his warmth. Maybe I can trust him too on what he has to say about God.

He speaks softly. "What your grandfather did to you was wrong. And so was what he said back there. You are not some mongrel. You are precious to God—and to me, even though I haven't known you long. If you need any help working through all this, you can call me day or night."

I drift off to sleep, my head still on his shoulder, and wake up only when Mom enters the chapel. I vaguely remember Coach driving us both home and climbing into bed, but I don't wake up again until my room is filled with sunlight the next day.

At first, I'm confused why I'm just waking up at 10:20 a.m., but then it all comes flooding back. A cloud settles over me. I climb out of bed and go downstairs. Mom, her eyes bloodshot, is at the table with a cup of coffee. She looks up at me.

I hate the taste of coffee, but I pour a cup just to have something to hold. I add several spoonfuls of sugar before I sit and wrap my hands around the mug.

Finally, I speak. "I guess it's over."

"All but the funeral."

"You're having a funeral for him? Are you kidding me? Don't plan on me going."

"Kiana, he is ... was my father. It's only right to have a service for him."

I stare into my mug, not daring to speak. I already know nothing I say will make a difference. She can make me go to the funeral, but she can't make me grieve for my grandfather. The only thing I have to grieve is my lost childhood.

I sip my coffee. It doesn't taste as bad as I expect. My thoughts turn toward the events of yesterday. I did get one good thing out of all this ... a dad.

Right now, all I want to do is freerun, but it's daytime, and I rarely freerun during the day. Besides, it's Wednesday, and Thorn is at school. I may as well go too. I go upstairs, dress, and grab my backpack.

"Where are you going?" Mom calls.

"School."

"You don't have to go today. You're excused."

"I want to go. I need to go."

"At least let me get dressed and drive you."

"I'm already late. I'll walk."

I close the door behind me and jog down the road toward school. At least there I can be with Thorn and Coach. And school might distract me from the thoughts invading my mind.

Chapter Twenty-Eight

I wake Monday morning to a sunny sky. My grandfather's funeral service is at 10:00 a.m., so Mom lets me sleep in. When I get up, I shower and pull on my best pair of jeans and a long-sleeved, white, button-up shirt. It's mid-April, so it'll be hot by noon, but I feel chilled, probably more from emotions than the weather.

We drive to Shady Glen Cemetery. Mom was going to have my grandfather cremated, but it turns out he had already purchased a lot at Shady Glen and paid for the burial.

We pull into the cemetery, and Mom navigates the narrow roads to a spot near the back. Each section of the cemetery is landscaped with lush green grass and a statue in the center. The statue in my grandfather's section is of a man and woman at a well. I walk closer to read the inscription: "But whoever drinks of the water I give him will never thirst." I guess that's from the Bible. I can ask Thorn or Coach later.

Mom and I walk over to where the pastor from Thorn's church is standing. Mom has asked him to do a graveside service. Hearing the sound of car doors being shut, I turn to see Thorn and his grandparents.

The day is too beautiful to be gathered at a cemetery. We sit in folding chairs arranged in front of my grandfather's casket. The hole to bury him has already been dug, and the ground is waiting to swallow him up. I feel movement beside me and turn. Coach takes a seat in the empty chair next me. Now Thorn is on one side, and Coach on the other. If only we were somewhere else doing something else.

Thorn's pastor opens a slim, leather-bound Bible and starts to read: "The Lord is my shepherd, I shall not want." Then the pastor reads verses about God preparing a place for us in heaven. He says a few words, prays, and it's over.

I blow out a stream of air. I'm not sure how I feel—glad this is over or angry that my grandfather should have a funeral like this.

He was a mean, evil man. He didn't deserve Scripture read over him or prayers as though he had faith in God like Coach does. What he did destroyed my parent's dreams and their relationship. Over fifteen years went by before they could find their way back to each other, and who knows whether or not they will get back together permanently. They are both different people than they were at eighteen.

And then there's me. He robbed me of my childhood. I can never get the past nine years back. Now the three of us have to figure out how to overcome the damage he did and move forward to forge new relationships and dream new dreams.

When the service is over, Mom walks to the casket. There's an arrangement of flowers on it, and she pulls out a flower and holds it against her chest. Is she thinking of happier times with her dad? Were there any? I should join her. She needs my emotional support. But I can't do it. My feet won't move that direction. I turn and walk away. Thorn follows. His grandparents and Coach join my mom graveside. She'll be okay.

I'm glad to get back into the routine of school and track practice, but the fact that Coach is my dad is never far from my mind. In a way, it helps because I push harder so I won't let him down. Other times, it distracts me. Thorn once asked me if I ever wondered if my dad was a runner. Now I know. He was.

A few days after the funeral, I stay after track practice to talk to him. He's easier to talk to than Mom. We were all affected by what my grandfather did, but in different ways.

I sit next to Coach on the bleachers. "Now that my grandfather is dead, I want to move on, but I don't know how to deal with what happened to me—to all of us really. I've always felt like I could never be normal. He stole normal from me. Now he's gone, and I'm tired of letting what he did affect me. You and Thorn both talk about God like he's a real person who has a purpose for everything. I wish I could believe it."

He nods. "I understand. Sometimes you simply have to accept things in faith. Accept you're not only created in a beautiful way by God, but that he has a plan for your life. Don't ask me why God doesn't stop people like your grandfather from doing hateful things, because I can't tell you that. I don't know why God didn't keep my brother Gerald from doing drugs or my dad from getting killed. For one, God gives people a choice, and sometimes we have to live with the bad choices other people make as well as our own.

He looks at me intently, and I can see in his eyes he really believes every word he's said. "I don't have to understand everything God does or doesn't do. I only have to trust that God loves me—all of us—and he knows what he's doing. He can use even the ugly things to make us stronger. God didn't stop all the bad things from happening in my own life, but I know now he was with me through all of it."

I shake my head. "I don't feel strong. I don't feel like there's any kind of plan for me."

"Don't be afraid to tell God that. You can be a victim and let it hold you back all your life, or you can face it and change things. Become a survivor. You can't change what happened to you, but you can decide it won't steal one more day of your life. I have to do the same."

Thorn is still waiting for me, so I get up to go. Coach pulls me into a hug, and I hug him back. I want to be a survivor, but I have no clue what that looks like.

Chapter Twenty-Nine

It's after midnight, and I'm too restless to sleep. I pull a hoodie over my T-shirt and pull on my high tops. I carefully ease the window up and slip into the night. The stars fill me with a sense of awe.

I start jogging around our block, but I add in freerunning moves. I speed-vault over the bench at the bus stop, then go back and do a reverse vault over it. I run as far as the convenience store and hit the wall, in and out, at a forty-five-degree angle. I jump to the top of the dumpster, ignoring the smell of rotted food, then run the edge to the other end and flip off it. I finish with a speed-vault over a sawhorse marking a large pothole and head back the house.

Climbing the porch post, I sit on the roof, and gaze into the night sky. I try to picture a God who actually knows about me and my problems. "Are you up there?" I ask. "If you are, I sure could use some help figuring things out down here."

There's no voice, no shooting stars or other sign, but my mind stills. I take a deep breath and slowly release it. Is this what peace feels like? I sit under the canopy of stars until I feel chilled, then climb back through the window. Dropping on my bed, I fall into a dreamless sleep. When I wake up in the morning, I know what I have to do.

Coach dismisses track practice early because it starts to drizzle, but he motions me over before I leave. I jog up to him. "When the track season is over, let's plan a day to do something together," he says.

I look at him. "Like what?"

He grins. "Dad-daughter stuff. What do you like to do?"

I shrug. "I never do much of anything but homework or freerunning."

"I know a freerun gym a couple of hours from here. Would you like to try it? We could leave early, freerun at the gym for a while, then see a movie or grab a pizza—or both. Does that sound good?"

I bite my bottom lip.

He tilts his head and looks at me. "What?"

"I'm still getting used to the idea of having a dad."

He clasps his hands behind his back and grins. "Really? Because I'm liking the idea of you being my daughter."

I feel my ears turning red. He puts his arm around my shoulder for a one-armed hug. Coach Clark is watching from across the track. She knows. I can see it on her face. But maybe she knew all along. Soon, everyone will know, but I don't care. I think having a dad is going to be really cool, and I tell him so. He squeezes me tighter. "Need a ride home?"

I shake my head. "No, there's something I need to do."

The drizzle has turned into a light rain as I climb into Thorn's truck. He pulls out of the lot and navigates the wet streets, wipers squeaking in protest. He reaches over and takes my hand but doesn't say anything. We don't need words. We both understand. He enters the open iron gates at Shady Glen and follows the narrow road to the back of the cemetery. I look for Jesus and the woman at the well. I know I can find it from there.

Thorn pulls off the side of the road. I climb out, leaving him in the truck. I have to do this alone. I head to the spot where fresh dirt indicates a new grave. The stone has been delivered, marking the spot. The rain has slowed to a drizzle.

I kneel in the wet soil and read "Walter Scott, Rest in Peace." Other tombstones say, "Beloved Husband and Father" or "Remembered in Love," but those descriptions don't fit my grandfather. For a brief moment, I wish I knew what happened to make him who he was. But that feeling passes as the familiar anger takes over.

Dampness seeps through my pants. The tears come. Not for

him, but for me. For the innocent childhood he stole from me. For the years I can never get back. For the relationship I never had with him or my grandmother. Or even my father until now. For the hours spent running from the visions that haunted me. For the way the things he did defined who I was.

I reach out and trace the W in his name with my finger. "I never really knew you. You were never a grandparent to me. The things you did to me should never be done to any child, much less by a grandfather." I stop. What good is saying all this? There's no one to listen. Still, I continue. For me.

"You could have loved me. Could have made me feel safe. But you hurt me. You hurt my mother. My father. Every life you touched, you blemished. But I refuse to let you rob me of any more of my life. I refuse to let you define my hopes and my dreams."

The drizzle stops, and the sky begins to clear. I remain kneeling on the ground, chilled from the dampness. "Your life is over and can't be redone, but my life is just beginning. I will live so my life will have meaning. I will make a difference. I will make the lives of others better. When I die, I want my tombstone to say, 'She was loved. She mattered.'"

I stay kneeling another minute. Sunshine peeks through the clouds, and a rainbow fills the sky. It's almost too cliché. Too obvious to ignore.

I look to the sky. "Is that you, God? Are you telling me there is a plan for me? That I am special to you no matter what has happened to me?"

I feel a sense of conflict in my spirit. Coach said I could tell God anything, so I do. "God, I don't understand why you let me save Isabella, but you didn't save me. Still, I accept that you do love me. Coach says you were with him during all he went through, and I need you to get me through what's ahead. Take the loss and somehow turn it around for good. Help me find the plan that Coach and Thorn say you have for me."

There's no answer except the peace that creeps into my heart. I smile as I choose to accept it as a promise of a hope-filled future.

I stand, turn my back on the grave, and walk to the truck. I doubt I'll be back.

Thorn is writing in his school notebook as I approach. He looks up in surprise when I open the door. "Step out," I tell him.

He does, and I point out the rainbow. "That's for me. For new beginnings."

Thorn takes my hand in his. "And for me. For new beginnings. I've written my father a letter. Said the things I've needed to say. Whatever happens with him, I feel ready to face it."

He opens the truck door, and I climb in. Then he climbs in his side. Silently, we leave the cemetery. Everything looks the same, yet nothing is the same for either of us.

I can never get back what I lost. And I'm still running , but I'm not running to escape nor to silence the voices in my head and the images that still haunt me. I'm running now for me. For my team. For Coach, my dad. For pure joy. Not just freerunning, but running free. Bad days may still come, but I won't look back. Only ahead. I'm writing my new ending. Today and tomorrow—and all the tomorrows that come after. I'm running toward my future and all I can be.

Notes:
This book is fiction, but many girls like Kia are molested or abused every day, the majority of them by someone they know, even someone who is a close family member. Kia dealt with it by running to escape the memories, but that's not the best option. If you are being harmed in any way, tell someone. If they don't believe you or don't help, tell someone else. Talk to a school counselor, pastor, police officer or social worker from your local social services office.

About the author:

Kathy grew up in northern Indiana, lived in three different continents while her husband was in the USAF, and now lives in the Florida Panhandle. She and her husband have eight children, five of whom are adopted, three from Haiti and two from the United States. They also have six grandchildren. Kathy's favorite activities are those that involve traveling and adventures that include her children and grandchildren.

In order to better relate to the characters in her stories, Kathy has done things such as whitewater rafting, certify in scuba diving, and get her motorcycle endorsement. She draws the line at sky diving.

Don't Miss
Catching Hope
by Kathy Cassel

Chapter One

The sound of a horn startled me awake. I struggled to a sitting position, excitement pulsing through me. I was in a large van sitting between my sixteen-year-old adoptive brother, Chad, and Levi, my twin, who were both still asleep. I nudged Levi until he opened his eyes and sat up. His red hair, a shade darker than mine, was tousled, and his sapphire blue eyes were sleepy. It had been a long drive from the airport to our resort on the Haitian coastline, and although I'd wanted to stay awake and take in the scenery, I drifted off.

Now we were stopped outside an ornate iron gate. Juvens, our driver, honked again, and a man in a uniform pushed a button triggering a motor to open the gate, allowing Juvens to pull through.

I turned to Levi. "Can you believe it? Us in a foreign country?"

He nodded but was silent. Handling new situations and the stress of unfamiliar places is hard for my twin. Until a year ago, Levi and I were bounced from foster home to foster home, never getting a forever family partly because Levi does things that make him stand out as different. The Michaels call it quirks of his autism, but other families weren't so understanding. In fact, they could be downright mean at times.

Right after our fourteenth birthday, our case manager moved Levi to a group home to help him transition into successful adult life. What really happened was he was targeted and ended up in the emergency room, where he first met Dr. Michaels. I met Dr. Michaels during the investigation into Levi's abuse. Then the Michaels decided to add us to their family.

After many discussions, accelerated training classes, and tons of paperwork, we were adopted. Dr. and Mrs. Michaels became our parents, and in the deal, we got a brother—Chad. He was adopted by the Michaels when he was six. Now he's sixteen, a year older than us. His skin is the color of caramel, and he's strong from all the sports he plays.

Our cousin Jen was in the seat in front of me next to Mrs. M. Jen is almost seventeen. Dr. Michaels and her dad, also known as Dr. Michaels, are brothers. She isn't adopted, and she let us know the first time we met. Thankfully, she lives in Michigan, and we live in the Florida panhandle, so it's not like we hang out much.

Even after the flight from Miami and the long van ride, her blond hair was pulled up in a perfect top knot. I made a mental note to ask Mrs. M to help me do something with my wild tangle of red hair once we were settled in.

Jen scowled. "I don't know why I had to come on this trip. I would have been fine staying home alone while my parents went on their trip to Europe—their vacation which didn't include their only child."

Dr. M turned from the front passenger seat. "You'll have to take that up with your parents. They evidently wanted to spend time alone. And they thought this trip would be a good experience for you." He smiled.

Jen didn't return his smile. She stuck her earphones back into her ears, seemingly not as curious about our new accommodations as I was.

Juvens drove slowly through the resort. Small, white houses with yellow trim and blue shutters were set among palm trees. In the middle of the resort, four small swimming pools were situated around a central concrete island filled with dirt. Lush palm trees were planted in the ornamental island.

"This is where we're staying? In one of those little houses?" I could hear the wonder in my voice, and Jen didn't miss it even with headphones in.

"Bungalows," she said. "Not little houses."

"Little houses. Bungalows. Same thing," Chad said. "Who cares anyway? Look at the sea."

I followed Chad's gaze. Waves were rolling in and crashing

onto a white sand beach, stretching as far as I could see. Chad's eyes devoured the water. "I can't wait to try out those waves!"

Juvens pulled in front of a bungalow, climbed out, and walked to the back of the van. He opened the back doors where our luggage was stored. As I went to get my luggage, a movement outside the fence drew my gaze. A short, thin man with skin like dark chocolate, a white scar etched above his right eye, was watching us. He focused on Dr. M, and his eyes narrowed, a look of pure hatred filling his face. His eyes met mine, and the look of fury on his face made my heart race. I quickly turned away. Who was the man? And more importantly, why was he looking at us as though he hated us?

CATCHING HOPE

A young adult novel by

Kathy Cassel

Newly adopted Lexi Michaels is taking her first real vacation as she, twin brother Levi, adoptive brother Chad, and new cousin Jen head to Haiti where their dad, a pediatrician, will be volunteering in an island clinic.

But who is the man who displays such hatred for the Michaels when they arrive at their resort? Is an attempted burglary as random as it appears? Will Jen ever accept the newcomers to the family?

When the four teens set out to explore Haiti's sights and history on their own, an unexpected encounter and natural disaster plunge them into adventure and danger. With their very survival at stake, can the four teens work together, or will Lexi's dream of a "forever family" end in tragedy?

**Available Now
at
Amazon.com**